W9-CGR-817

PINE HILL BOARD OF EDUCATION
1003 TURNERVILLE ROAD
PINE HILL, NEW JERSEY 08021

THE
SINGING TREE

WRITTEN AND ILLUSTRATED BY

KATE SEREDY

PUFFIN BOOKS

PUFFIN BOOKS

Published by the Penguin Group

Penguin Books USA Inc., 375 Hudson Street, New York, New York 10014, U.S.A.

Penguin Books Ltd, 27 Wrights Lane, London W8 5TZ, England

Penguin Books Australia Ltd, Ringwood, Victoria, Australia

Penguin Books Canada Ltd, 10 Alcorn Avenue, Toronto, Ontario, Canada M4V 3B2

Penguin Books (N.Z.) Ltd, 182-190 Wairau Road, Auckland 10, New Zealand

Penguin Books Ltd, Registered Offices: Harmondsworth, Middlesex, England

First published in the United States of America by the Viking Press, 1939
Published in Puffin Books 1990
9 10 8

LIBRARY OF CONGRESS CATALOGING IN PUBLICATION DATA

Seredy, Kate.   The singing tree / by Kate Seredy.   p.   cm.
Summary: Life changes drastically for a Hungarian family when
World War I upsets their peaceful, contented existence and the
children are left in charge of the farm.
ISBN 0-14-034543-4
[1. World War, 1914-1918—Hungary—Fiction.   2. Farm life—
Fiction.   3. Hungary—Fiction.]   I. Title.
PZ7.S48Si   1990   [Fic]—dc20   90-35977

Printed in the United States of America
Set in Garamond #3

TO MY FATHER

CONTENTS

LIST OF FULL-PAGE DRAWINGS

LIST OF FULL-PAGE DRAWINGS

THE SINGING TREE

CHAPTER I

UNCLE MOSES

UNCLE MOSES took off his small black skullcap and wiped his forehead. Grimy fingers left black smudges on his silvery hair and came away wet from perspiration. He rubbed them absent-mindedly against his black alpaca smock, while he gazed at the crowded shelves in his crowded store.

Outside the sun was shining; the long village street was gay with freshly whitewashed houses and blooming geraniums in the blue and green windowboxes. The air was fragrant with late acacia blossoms; the whole village was resounding with the laughter of playing children, mixed with the cackling of

13

hens, the honk-honk of waddling geese, the yips and barks of dogs. But the sunshine, the fragrance, colors, and sounds of June did not penetrate into the dim, crowded store. Here the dusty smell of bolts of dressgoods mingled with the smells of cheese, salted herring, machine oil, kerosene, harness leather, peppermint candies, bacon and sausages, all spiced with the odor of marjoram, dried pepper, anise, and garlic.

Outside in the sunshine, thousands of bees droned happily, gathering honey from the clusters of acacia blossoms. Inside, Uncle Moses went to work again among the clusters of pepper, spices, and sausages hanging from the ceiling, humming a tuneless little song that sounded just like the happy droning of the bees. He moved here and there, between crates and barrels, piles of plowshares and shovels, rows of shoes, boxes filled with ribbons, toys, candles. Now and then he poked at a bunch of mixed merchandise. "Ho-hum-la-la," he hummed. "Two dozen pocketknives . . . hmmm-hmmm . . . three bolts red percale . . . ho-hum-mmm." He squeezed his small, bent frame into every nook and cranny, looked at all the shelves, peered into half-empty barrels and boxes, poked at piles of junk. Finally he opened a small door in the back of the store and disappeared, closing the door behind him.

The store was empty for a few minutes, then the bell of the street door jangled and a boy stuck his head in.

"Uncle Mo!" he called. No one answered, so he opened the door wider.

"Uncle Moses, where are you?"

"He isn't here, Kate," he said over his shoulder.

"He has *got* to be here. Uncle Moses is always in the store," declared Kate with conviction, pushing him inside.

"Uncle Mo, where are you? We want some red satin ribbon."

"I don't!" exclaimed the boy indignantly. "I want to go home and milk the cows. You girls with your ribbons and laces and fancy clothes—wasting my time waiting in stores for hours."

"Hours, indeed!" retorted Kate. "We just stepped in a moment ago—why, the bell is still jingling! Besides, who is so particular about ribbons and flowers on his hat? *You* are, my dear cousin Jancsi!" She pointed an accusing finger at him.

"Well, anyway"—he evaded the point—"Uncle Mo isn't here, so we can go home. Come on, Kate."

"Not without my red satin ribbon, I won't," said Kate, seating herself on top of a keg with the air of someone who is going to stay there until she gets her way. She spread her pleated skirts around her, dug her small fists into her waist, and the way she looked at him out of sparkling, mischievous eyes, spelled: "What are you going to do about it?" He answered the challenge by making a determined move as if to carry her off by force, but it came to nothing because the little door in the back creaked open and Uncle Moses emerged. He was covered with cobwebs and his wrinkled old face had a preoccupied look. For a moment he didn't see them but kept on humming:

"Hmmm-la-la-la, stock up on wool and tanned leather . . . wool and leather. . . ."

Kate began to laugh. "Uncle Moses, what in the world are you doing?"

"Kate . . . and Jancsi!" cried Uncle Moses, hurrying forward as fast as the boxes, crates, and barrels would let him. "This is a pleasure, to see you in my store. Sit down, Jancsi."

"We are in a hurry, Uncle Mo," said Jancsi. "Give her those pink or red frills she wants," he added gruffly, "so I can get home to work. You know Father . . ."

Uncle Moses smiled. "Yes, indeed I know him. And so do you, Jancsi. He wouldn't hurt a fly, let alone his only son."

Jancsi squirmed. "That's just it. He left this morning for the corrals and he told me to harrow the corn and do the milking before sundown, and I started to until *this*"—he jerked a derisive thumb toward Kate—"started to yowl into Mother's ear for red satin ribbons and . . . here we are. Father will just look at the corn and then look at me and then I'll feel like a . . . worm or something. Will you hurry up now?" he almost shouted at Kate.

Kate settled herself more firmly on the keg. "He is just jealous, Uncle Mo, because Auntie is making a new bonnet for me with bought ribbons and he can't have any for his hat. But tell me," she hurried on with an impish glance at her spluttering cousin, "tell me, what have you been doing back there? Just look at your nice black coat, all covered with dust and cobwebs!"

"Looking over my stock, taking inventory," said Uncle Moses, rubbing cobwebs off his shoulders. He peered at Kate over his glasses. "That means . . ."

"I know what it means. Daddy showed us how to keep books; remember, Jancsi? He wanted Uncle Márton to keep books on the horses and sheep and everything, but he wouldn't."

"Of course not. He doesn't need books to tell him what he has. He can count the beasts he sells, and who could count them on the range, I'd like to know!" snapped Jancsi.

"You keep books, don't you, Uncle Mo?" asked Kate.

"Not on paper. In here," replied Uncle Moses, smiling and pointing to his forehead. "This is the only safe place to keep records in. Safe from fire or nosy people or gnawing mice."

"Don't you ever forget anything?" asked Kate, slightly mollified.

"How could I? I was brought up in this store, so was my father and his father before him. I can lay my hands on anything in this store . . . with my eyes closed."

Even Jancsi looked dubious now. Horses and sheep were different; it was easy to remember where to find them because they were fenced in at the corrals or pastures and that was all there was to it. But to remember all these different, strange things. . . . He couldn't quite believe that.

"*Anything*, Uncle Mo? Supposing I wanted to buy . . ." He looked around, trying to think of something he couldn't see in the store, when the doorbell jingled and a young man walked in.

"Uncle Mo," he said importantly after waving a casual greeting at Kate and Jancsi, "I want the very best coat buttons there are in the world. A full dozen of them!"

"Silver buttons!" cried Jancsi, looking triumphantly at Uncle Mo. "Supposing he wanted to buy silver buttons, where would you find them?"

"On the top shelf by the window, in a little box behind the mousetraps," said Uncle Mo without a moment's hesitation. "Fetch them for me, Jancsi; you are younger than I am. Just step on this nail-keg here. Way back in the corner . . . that's the one!"

He took the box from Jancsi, blew the thick gray dust from the cover and opened it. "The very best silver buttons there are in the world . . . maybe" (he whispered the "maybe") "a full dozen of them!" He took one carefully from its bed of white cotton, rubbed it on his sleeve, then held it up in the slanting sunlight, watching the young man's face.

"Just the thing for a new blue coat, Peter—for a wedding . . . maybe?"

Peter's eyes were shining. "Red and green stones in it, too! Sure it's for my wedding, but"—his face fell—"I can't afford silver buttons. I need a cow."

Uncle Mo folded his hands and peered at him sideways.

"How many sheep have you got now, Peter?"

"Why . . . why . . . about forty," stammered Peter, who couldn't see the connection between buttons and sheep, let alone the cow.

"Forty." Uncle Moses nodded, then he lifted his eyes to the ceiling and mumbled rapidly to himself. "I could"—he turned to Peter again—"I could sell you a nice, gentle cow for the wool off forty sheep and throw in the buttons for good measure." He gave the button another vigorous rub and held it against his black coat.

"Mmmm . . . isn't it beautiful? Well, what do you say, Peter?"

"It has got to be a good milker . . ." hesitated Peter, staring at the glittering button.

"Good," nodded Uncle Moses, for whom the sale was concluded. "Here are the buttons. You can come for the cow tomorrow and deliver the wool as soon as you get around to shearing. And now what else can I do for you?"

"I . . . well, I guess that's all. . . . I don't need anything else," faltered Peter.

"Leave it to me . . . I know you do. New boots . . . something for Mari . . . perhaps a new harness for the team . . ." suggested Uncle Moses.

"No. Can't sell me a thing, Uncle Mo. Good-by." Peter marched out. He was half-way to his team and wagon when the voice of Uncle Moses floated after him: "Jancsi, tell your father that the new brass-studded harness I ordered came in yesterday. It's a shame to drive a good team with that old, patched-up harness. What will people say?"

Peter stopped in his tracks. There was only one team in sight, his own. He looked back at Uncle Moses, who was standing in the doorway, apparently not paying any attention to him.

"What's wrong with this harness?" he called. Uncle Moses turned around, looking very innocent. "Oh, it's your team, Peter? Well, you could oil it up maybe . . . for the wedding you know . . . or maybe people wouldn't notice the mended parts anyway, looking at your silver buttons on the new blue coat. Some might say that you are thinking more of yourself than of your bride . . . taking her home behind a team with old harness on and all, but . . . I wouldn't pay any attention to gossip."

Peter was back in the store. "Where is that new harness you ordered for Mr. Nagy?" he demanded.

"Why . . . it's hanging right behind the door there, Peter. Complete with brass studs, tassels, and all. Just look at it. Good enough even for Mr. Nagy's black team, huh? Takes a first-class team to show off trappings like that."

"So? Well, I've got as good a team as anybody around here," bragged Peter. "How much?" he asked, fingering the harness.

Uncle Moses rubbed his nose thoughtfully, then came back with another question: "How much money did you say you had saved up for a cow?"

"Two hundred pengö," said Peter absent-mindedly, patting his pocket.

"Mmm, mmm." Uncle Moses shook his head in disapproval. "That's an awful lot of money for just a plain cow. Why, this harness with all the brass and things costs only one hundred and ninety-five. This is your lucky day, Peter. You come to Uncle Moses for buttons and you get a cow and a new harness *and* a dozen silver buttons."

"But . . . I didn't . . ." Peter began, but Uncle Moses, by some sleight-of-hand, had fished a braided carriage whip from behind his back. "And this beautiful whip as a gift . . . *if* you pay cash for the harness now." He finished the sentence as

if Peter hadn't spoken. "Jancsi will help carry the harness to your wagon . . . won't you, Jancsi?"

"Huh? . . . Oh . . . yes, yes, of course," stammered Jancsi, absorbed in Uncle Moses' salesmanship. Watching and listening, he had completely forgotten about going home, corn, cows, and everything.

"I don't need any help, thanks," grumbled Peter, reaching for the harness.

"You don't want the whip?" asked Uncle Moses gently.

"Sure I do. Here . . . fifty, one hundred . . . and ninety-five . . ." he counted the money into Uncle Mo's palm. He grinned at Jancsi. "Tell Mr. Nagy that I saw the harness first! And . . . you must all come to dance at my wedding. You too, Uncle Moses."

"Whew!" sighed Jancsi when the door slammed after Peter. "Uncle Moses, this is too much for me. Buttons . . . cow . . . wool, harness, whip . . . how do you keep all this straight? Where will you get the cow and . . . Uncle Mo"—he wagged a finger accusingly—"*did* my father order a new harness?"

"Did I say he had?" chuckled Uncle Moses, spreading out his hands.

"You said for me to tell Father . . . oh . . ." Jancsi began to laugh, "I remember now. Oh, Uncle Moses, you are funny!"

"Well, he did need a new harness," giggled Kate. "Uncle Mo, have you got a cow too somewhere in a little box behind the mousetraps?"

Uncle Mo shook his head. He had a far-away look in his eyes. "You know for whom I had ordered those buttons?

Seventeen years ago," he went on, "a handsome young man came in here and said: 'Uncle Mo, I want a dozen of the very best buttons, silver buttons for my wedding suit.' I ordered two dozen for him to choose from; twelve with blue and red stones, twelve with green and red. He took the dozen with the blue and red stones because, he said, 'the blue stones sparkled like the eyes of my sweetheart and the red stones glowed like the love in my heart'."

"What a nice thing to say!" said Kate. "Who was he?"

"His name is Márton Nagy."

"Father! Uncle Márton!" exclaimed Kate and Jancsi together.

Uncle Mo smiled. "And I have kept the other dozen behind the mousetraps ever since."

"Did you sell him a cow and harness and a whip too?" giggled Kate. Uncle Mo let this go unanswered. He was thinking of something else, because he was scratching the end of his nose. "Jancsi . . . would you do an errand for me?"

"Of course, Uncle Mo."

"Run over to the Vidor farm and tell old János Vidor that I would like to see him . . . on business."

While Jancsi was gone, Kate selected the red satin ribbon she wanted. "This is for the new bonnet I am to wear at Peter's wedding," she explained. Uncle Moses was just wrapping it up when Jancsi returned, followed by János Vidor. He edged inside, twisting his weatherbeaten hat between his hands.

"Uncle Mo . . . if you want me to pay that bill . . . I just haven't got the money."

"Now, now, János, who is thinking of money?" soothed Uncle Moses. "Young Nagy here was speaking about a cow, wondering where I could get a good, gentle one. Weren't you, Jancsi?"

"Sure, I wanted to know how . . ." Jancsi began to explain, but Uncle Mo raised his voice: "So I thought of you, János. Now that your daughter is getting married, I thought maybe you would want to sell that brown cow of yours . . . maybe."

"Well . . . I kind of figured on giving it to Mari for a wedding present," hesitated János Vidor.

"Peter has bought a cow for her already, a good milker too. He was here a little while ago," remarked Uncle Moses, gazing intently at the ceiling. "But I could pay you a hundred and fifty pengö for that cow today."

János looked up, interested. Uncle Moses bent forward and tapped him on the chest with one finger. "And we'll forget about that old bill, János."

János was visibly weakening, but Uncle Moses wasn't through yet. "Then you could maybe buy those fancy thin glasses Mari has her heart set on. For a wedding present and only fifteen pengö for a full dozen with the pitcher besides."

"I could, at that!" smiled János. Uncle Moses was already counting out part of the money he had received from Peter. "There. Now you don't owe me anything, János, and there are the glasses all wrapped up nicely in the box behind you."

"Thank you, Uncle Moses, thank you. Mari will sure be happy with these." János Vidor was backing out with the package held tenderly in his arms.

"Don't mention it. Bring the cow over tonight after milking . . . and don't break those glasses!"

When the door closed, he turned to Kate, chuckling. "Books! Do I need books, I ask you?"

Jancsi was frowning. "Uncle Mo, I can't understand this. I . . . I am dizzy. You sold Peter a cow you didn't have for wool he hasn't sheared yet, a harness for the money he should have paid for the cow, then you bought the cow János was going to give them anyway. . . . My saints, it's all mixed up!"

Uncle Moses sat down next to Jancsi on the crate. Dressed in shiny black from head to toes, with his hunched shoulders and long, heavy nose, he looked like a benevolent old crow. He peered at Jancsi with his head cocked sideways.

"You don't think I was very honest . . . is that it, Jancsi?"

"Well"—Jancsi blushed a deep red, because that was just what had worried him—"I don't understand. . . ."

"Because you don't know these people as well as I do. Look. Peter is a good, honest farmer but he is young and a little reckless. He has a lot of friends in the village, single men of his own age who have been expecting a big party before he got married. The two hundred pengö was burning a hole in his pocket. . . . I could see that when he came in. It would have been spent, with nothing but a headache to show for it.

"Now he has a cow, the harness, a whip . . . and five pengö left. Old János has the money—he needs it too—Mari has the glasses, I have the wool . . . *and* a little profit. So"—he spread out his hands—"everybody is happy."

"That's wonderful, Uncle Moses!" cried Kate. "But how do you figure it all out so fast?"

"Not fast, Kate," smiled Uncle Moses. "I sit here in the store all day, year after year. All my life. And I watch, I listen. They all come to me; I sell them wedding gifts, baby rattles, funeral shrouds. I sell them food, furniture, clothing. I don't have to go to their houses to know what they need; they don't have to tell me when they are hard up; I know it when the bills begin to grow that there is trouble. Then I begin to do the thinking and worrying for them, just as my father and grandfather did before me. They are young, these children of the soil, their youth is renewed every spring with the fresh green plants and the new-born animals. Strong, young, healthy, but they don't like to think about money. We Jews are weak, Jancsi, and we were born old. But in here"—he tapped his forehead again—"in here lies our strength."

Kate bent forward and laid a hand gently on his heart: "And in here, Uncle Moses?"

"Well," the old man smiled, "I make money using my brains and lose money listening to my heart. But in the long run my books balance pretty well."

The hoarse, plaintive sound of a cowherder's horn broke the short silence, and Jancsi jumped. "Good heavens, Kate, the cows are coming in! Let's get home, or Father will forget that I'm thirteen years old and give me . . . more than a look. Good-by, Uncle Moses!" He turned back from the open door to grin at him. "And I think you're—all right!" He rushed out, shouting for Kate to follow. Before she left, she bent and shyly kissed the withered face of the old merchant. "Bless you, Uncle Moses," she whispered and hurried out.

Uncle Moses, alone in the dusty store, rose slowly to his feet. He looked up, far beyond the peppers, spices, and sausages on the ceiling, and spoke to someone there, reverently: "Thank Thee for children like these."

 CHAPTER II

THE POPLAR LANE

WHEN Kate reached the wagon that had been waiting behind the store, Jancsi had already unhitched the horses. "Now we're in for it." He frowned at her. Kate didn't seem concerned. "Well, if we are, we might as well make the best of it. Tell you what," she cried, struck by an idea, "we might stop at the schoolhouse and see if Daddy is still there. He was to come home today—last day of school, you know—and if we take him home, maybe Uncle Márton won't notice the corn."

"And maybe you're wrong, as usual. He has already noticed the corn and now he is down by the brook looking for a fresh willow-switch. I can . . . I can feel it," said Jancsi wryly.

31

"If you can, then it's too late to worry. Here we go!" laughed Kate. Quick as lightning she had pulled the reins and given a healthy shriek at the same time. The wagon jerked forward, turned down the narrow lane leading to the school-house, and before Jancsi could gather his wits about him they were in the midst of a swarm of shouting, laughing village children. Boys and girls were just leaving the schoolyard, push-ing through the gate in tight bunches and scattering, in an incredibly short time, into near-by farmyards, gardens, and over the surrounding fields.

"Shoo!" cried Kate, flapping her hands at them. "Shoo, baby chicks, back to your coops! Daddy! Dad-dyyy!" she yelled in the same breath, noticing her father in the doorway. "Come on home with us. Jancsi is *scared!*"

"You keep quiet, you . . . screaming monkey, you. Who is scared?" shouted Jancsi. He waved to Kate's father. "Hurry, Uncle Sándor, school is over!"

Sándor Nagy waved back, turned the big key in the lock, and hung it on a nail. He strode over to the wagon, dusting his hands. "Over for two whole months," he sighed happily. "I feel just like those youngsters; I could yell and turn cart-wheels in the dust.

"This is a pleasant surprise," he went on, seating himself between Kate and Jancsi. "I was planning to hire someone to drive me out and now I get a free ride."

"In good company." Kate grinned at him, hugging his arm. He lifted his eyebrows.

"I'll decide that after we get home. It seems to me I've

heard about one half of my good company having pushed the
other half off this very wagon onto this very, very dusty road."

"Oh . . . that happened when we were young, Daddy!"
interrupted Kate, casting an uneasy glance at Jancsi. She *had*
pushed him off and laughed at him and he still resented it.

"I see," said her father with a serious face. "And now I suppose you are quite an old lady?"

"Well, I'm almost thirteen, Daddy. Auntie has made three
extra petticoats for my holiday dress; that's only seven less
than she wears. And she said I could dance at Peter's wedding
. . . even with the big boys!"

"Aw, nobody'll want to dance with you," grumbled Jancsi.
"Wearing bought ribbons on your bonnet! Boys like girls
who make their own clothes."

"Do you, Jancsi?" asked Kate sweetly, peering at him from
under her downcast lashes.

"Sure. Any sensible man would."

"Then why," pounced Kate, "why did you follow that Lily
around, ogling her like a sick calf? 'Jancsi dear,' " she mimicked
in an affected voice, " 'there is a fly buzzing around me!
Jancsi dear, the sun is too hot. Jancsi dear, pray do not sit on
my dress!' Bah! It's a good thing she went back to that fine
finishing school in Budapest, or Jancsi dear would be still
chasing flies instead of doing his chores. And what's more,
Daddy," she rushed on as beet-red Jancsi tried to shush her
down, "what's more, he was tormenting Uncle Márton for
long black pants and shoes because that Lily said only peasants
wear pleated pants and boots. Just because her father is the

new judge and she goes to finishing school, she needn't put on airs!"

She paused, out of breath, and her father suppressed a laugh. "She is a little goose . . . but pretty! Isn't she, Jancsi?"

"I dunno," mumbled Jancsi. "I didn't look at her. Father said to be polite because she was a guest, so I was. Hey! Git up, there!" he yelled at the horses, cracking his whip. "I have wasted enough time without you crawling like snails! Git up!"

"What were you doing in the village, anyway?" asked Kate's father.

Jancsi only grunted, sending a withering glance at the tiny package in Kate's hand.

"Oh, Daddy, we had such a nice time!" she cried. "Did you know that Uncle Moses keeps books in his head and he could even remember that he had buttons behind the mouse-traps since Uncle Márton got married and now he sold them to Peter and gave him a cow that he . . . oh, no, it was the other way around. . . ."

"Hold on, chatterbox!" cried her father, laughing. "What books does Uncle Moses keep in his head?"

Little by little the children told him the story of the afternoon. Jancsi forgot his grudge too as he tried to explain the strange tactics of Uncle Moses. "He is awfully good, Uncle Sándor!" he finished, looking at his uncle with shining eyes. "And if that Lily ever calls him a nasty old Jew again, I'll just slap . . . well . . . pull her hair, anyway."

"Did she say that?" wailed Kate. "Ooooh, just let me hear her say it *once!* I'll fix those crimpy yellow curls of hers.

Why, Uncle Moses is the kindest, the best . . ." She choked with indignation, beating her small brown fists against her knee. For once Jancsi was in perfect accord with her. "She said 'Jew' as if that were something not nice. Why, Uncle Sándor?" he appealed to him.

"She said 'peasant' the same way too," gasped Kate.

Sándor Nagy looked from one angry little face to the other without speaking. Then he raised his eyes to the tall, ancient poplars lining the lane the wagon was just entering. Suddenly he said: "Jancsi, did your father ever tell you the story of this lane?"

"Why, no," said Jancsi in a puzzled voice. "Is there a story?"

"Stop the horses, Jancsi. I want to show you something and tell you a story. When you have heard that, you won't be angry at Lily any more; you'll only feel sorry for her because she is so stupid. Don't worry," he added, with a smile at Jancsi's doubtful look, "I'll take the blame for coming home late."

They walked back to the point where the poplar-lined lane joined the main road. There he stepped off the road into the mass of vines, underbrush, and tall grasses. He pushed aside the tangled growth. Leaning against the gray old trunk of the first tree stood an ancient carved post. Once deeply chiseled letters were still faintly visible on its face. Jancsi and Kate squeezed closer to read them.

"Liberty . . . equality . . . fraternity," Jancsi read slowly. "The . . . month of March 1848. And a lot of names. . . ."

"Look, Jancsi!" cried Kate. "The first name is Márton Nagy!"

"Father! Oh, no, it couldn't be, not in 1848 . . ." puzzled Jancsi, with his finger tracing the name.

"Your great-grandfather, children. Read the others too; most of them will sound familiar."

"János Vidor . . . Pál Hódi . . . Magyar . . ." read Kate, down the two long columns of names. "Reverend Bodor . . . and, oh, look! The last name is Moses Mandelbaum!"

"Yes," said her father seriously, "that's what I wanted you to see. This list of good Hungarians, beginning with Márton Nagy the large landowner and ending with Moses Mandelbaum, the small Jewish merchant. Between those two lies the past and the future of Hungary. As long as these two work together in peace and understanding, little harm can come to the country. We are all dependent on these two: the farmer who grows food and the small merchant, the Jewish merchant who knows through centuries of scrimping and saving how to buy and sell wisely.

"The month of March in 1848 meant the beginning of this partnership, the dawn of a happy new era in Hungary. Feudal estates were divided into farms; peasants, who had been little more than slaves, were made into free men with the right to vote, marry, and travel as they pleased. People of the Jewish religion, who had been shamefully persecuted and oppressed for centuries, were once more free to trade and barter openly or to pursue any occupation they chose.

"Your great-grandfather Márton Nagy was one of the last great feudal landlords. Moses Mandelbaum, grandfather of Uncle Moses, was one of the first Jews who opened a store

under the new laws. And this avenue of trees"—he pointed ahead into the green lane—"had been planted in March 1848, one tree by every one of those whose names you have just read. The former master, who was one of his people now, all the peasants, who now were his equal in rights, and Moses Mandelbaum, they each planted a tree. A green, living thing to grow and remind them always that they were brother Hungarians, first and last."

He paused, looking ahead. The trees whispered in the light breeze; otherwise there was no sound. "Whispering trees," he went on gently as if speaking to them, "they have weathered many storms. Some of them are broken and almost dead, but new shoots are springing up from their roots every year. Those roots grow deep in the soil, deeper than the trees are tall. No one could kill them without destroying the very soil they grow in; what they stand for lives in the hearts of all Hungarians. Nothing could kill that without destroying the country."

"Gosh," breathed Jancsi, "I'm goose-pimples all over. "From Márton Nagy to Moses Mandelbaum," he said slowly, looking up and down the green lane. "I . . . I hope these trees will live forever."

"Just the same, if I ever hear that Lily laugh at Uncle Moses again," muttered Kate between her teeth, "I'll . . ."

Her father bent down and whispered something in her ear. She grinned. "With a willow-switch?"

"A fresh willow-switch." He grinned back, taking both children by the hand. "But if we don't hurry now, Brother will be angry enough to try it on all of us. Come on home!"

The farmyard was dark and quiet when the wagon drove in. Candles glowed in the windows of the house and a faint streak of light showed in the open barn. As the horses stopped, a shadow moved across the light. Jancsi's father was standing in the doorway. Jancsi couldn't see his face, but the way he stood there straight and silent, just sort of waiting, sent a shiver down his back.

"Father . . ." he began, nudging Uncle Sándor, who promptly came to his rescue.

"My fault, Márton. I've kept them out this late."

It didn't help. "Jancsi," came the stern voice of Father, "wash your hands and finish milking. Get going."

"Yes, Father." Jancsi was off the seat and in the barn in a flash. If he made rather a wide circle around Father, maybe nobody noticed it in the dark.

"Kate," spoke Father again, "your aunt needs help in the kitchen."

"Yes, Uncle Márton," gulped Kate and disappeared like a shadow.

"Yes, Brother," chuckled her father, "I'll do anything if only you'll spare me."

Márton Nagy laughed as they shook hands. "You can help me with these horses, Sándor, and . . . welcome home! Where have the little rascals been, anyway?"

The horses had been unspanned, brushed, and fed, and still the two brothers talked on. They didn't see each other very often. For years Kate's father has been a schoolteacher in Budapest. His wife had died there when Kate was nine years old and, as he sometimes laughingly referred to her, "the most impossible, incredible, headstrong little imp!" After he had nursed her through the measles and several tantrums, he had sent her to his brother's ranch for a short vacation. The vacation stretched to weeks, then months. When finally at Christmas time he came to visit her, he realized that Kate had changed. She was happy here, the ranch was where she belonged. Within a few days the old homestead had claimed him too; he gave up his job in the city and came to stay on the ranch.

Since then the old village schoolteacher had retired and Sándor had taken his place. The ranch was too far from the village for a daily trip, but at least he could spend all his vacation days with his family.

"Home! That's what this place is, Márton," he said now, stretching his arms wide as if he wanted to embrace the plains. "Home, as no place in the city can ever be. There you are always walled in like a prisoner, and your closest neighbors are strangers. Each family seems to live in a little cell, not knowing or caring what goes on next door. Here, miles of the plains separate us from the nearest neighbor and yet I feel among friends. I know that, should we really need help, they'd come from far and near, as we would go to them."

"Of course," said Márton Nagy with a smile in his voice. He had never known any other life; to him all this seemed as natural as the dark blue sky above. "We are one big family. We share the same joys and sorrows. Our life depends on what the land gives us; we pray together for rain in the spring, for sunshine at harvest time. We work and we play together; how else could we live?"

Jancsi hurried across the yard, carrying two full milkpails, and disappeared in the kitchen. Sándor Nagy looked after him and said: "I hope he will follow in your footsteps, Brother, and stay on the ranch."

"Jancsi? Why, you couldn't pry him loose! He knows this place almost better than I do. The way that boy can pick horses for breeding . . . well . . . I couldn't do it. I've been inspecting the new batch of foals at the corrals this afternoon. They're the best we've ever had."

Sándor Nagy laughed. "And he only thirteen, a young colt himself."

"Uhuh," chuckled Jancsi's father, "and I hold the reins . . . yet. But if anything happened to me, he could carry on."

"Few men could say that about their sons, Brother," said Sándor Nagy. "You certainly have a magic touch with young things. Just look at Kate! It's hard to believe that she is the same girl I sent to you only two years ago. She was a spoiled, willful, bad-tempered, skinny little imp and now . . ."

"Now she is a sturdy little imp with a very healthy temper when it's aroused," laughed Márton Nagy. "Let anyone interfere with her chicken business and she will tell you in no uncertain words to mind your own affairs!"

"What chicken business?" asked Kate's father, surprised.

"Didn't she tell you? She has full charge of the poultry yard and she makes those hens earn their keep or out they go. A regular egg factory!"

The kitchen door opened. "Suppe-e-e-er," called Jancsi's mother. "Welcome home, Sándor!" she greeted Kate's father cheerfully, then glanced anxiously at her husband's face. "Don't be angry with them," she whispered. He winked at her, then faced the room with a make-believe stern face.

The old kitchen was warm and cheerful in the candlelight, fragrant with the spicy smell of woodsmoke and baking food. Kate was bustling back and forth between the large white stove in the corner that looked like a huge beehive and the table. Jancsi appeared from the milk room, carrying two pitchers of foaming milk. He set them down on the table, took a very deep breath, and faced his father.

"Father, it was my fault . . ." he began, but Kate pushed him aside. "It was *not*, Uncle Márton. I asked him to . . ." She couldn't finish, either, because Mother said hurriedly, taking a stand between them:

"I gave them an errand to do."

"And I kept them out, telling stories," finished Sándor Nagy, making a fourth in the row. Father looked from one to another, then he began to laugh.

"So! I had to live to see my whole family line up against me. What am I . . . a dragon? Come on," he said, pushing them toward the table, "come on and eat your supper."

"But remember, Son"—he turned to Jancsi after they were seated—"you are a farmer. Leaving your job in the corn wasn't so bad. But, the first thing a *good* farmer learns is that when milking time comes, a cow isn't interested in excuses, good or bad. All a cow wants is to be milked."

"Yes, sir," gulped Jancsi, visibly relieved. He frowned into his plate, then glanced quickly at Father. Yes, the storm was over. He grinned.

"I am glad we aren't raising cows, anyway!"

"What's wrong with cows?" demanded Mother.

"Nothing. They are . . . well, they're just cows, that's all," grunted Jancsi. "All they do is eat and then bawl to be milked so they can eat some more. Horses now"—his face brightened—"horses are different! You can ride them, train them, talk to them. When you talk to a horse, his ears will stand up keen and sharp and he'll look at you smiling with his beautiful brown eyes, sort of saying: 'I know just what you mean.' Like you are looking now, Father." After a moment's silence a burst of laughter broke out and he blushed. "I mean . . ."

"Spoken like a good horseman, Jancsi," said Father, laughing. "I take it as a compliment."

"You mean that, Father?" cried Jancsi, forgetting his embarrassment. "You mean that I am a good horseman?"

Father was suddenly very busy with his supper. "Old Arpád thinks you are," he said casually.

"He does!" breathed Jancsi, looking around with eyes as big as saucers. Old Arpád was the most famous horse-herder in the whole country. Breeders and ranchers came to him for advice from far places.

"Yes," said Father, still not looking at his awe-struck son, "he seems to think that you are good enough to have your own herd."

Except for a little squeak of surprise from Kate, there was

no sound. Father reached for a piece of bread and began to spread butter on it slowly, carefully. Mother looked at Jancsi's tense little face and took pity on him . . . as always.

"Don't torment the boy, Márton. Tell him!" she cried.

"So they are fencing off a few acres for your herd, Son. You start with five mares and six foals."

"Six!" exclaimed Jancsi.

"The old chestnut had twins. Healthy little rascals. You can ride out in the morning to see them. After milking!" he shouted before his laughing voice was choked off by the small whirlwind that was Jancsi. He hugged his father with all his strength, thumped Uncle Sándor on the back, pulled Kate's pigtail, and landed a resounding kiss on Mother's cheek. She held him tight to her, so the ear-splitting whoop of joy Jancsi managed was partly muffled against her shoulder. Father had turned to Uncle Sándor, who was still coughing from the unexpected attack. "I am not experienced in business ways, Sándor," Father laughed. "Is it customary for a man who has been promoted to choke everybody in sight?"

"Well," said Uncle Sándor, pretending to be serious, "the more accepted procedure is to shake hands and make a speech."

Jancsi wriggled free of Mother's arms. He was flushed, his hair stood on end, but he tried to pull his face into serious lines.

"Thank you, Father," he said, holding out his hand. "I will try to . . . try to . . ." He gulped and blinked; speeches were not his strongest point.

"I know you will, Son. Shake on it," said Father, accepting, without the need of words, what Jancsi wanted to say. "And what are you sniffling about, old lady?" He turned to Mother, who was stealthily wiping her eyes on the corner of her apron.

"They grow so fast!" said Mother in a voice that shook a little, looking first at Jancsi, then at Kate. "Only a little while ago he was a baby." She smiled ruefully. "I feel the same way as when I watch the young swallows try their wings. Then it seems no time at all before they are ready to leave their nest. . . ."

"The mother swallow does not cry, though," said Father gently.

"Maybe not," sighed Mother, smiling through her tears. Jancsi laid his arms around her shoulder awkwardly. "Aw, Mother, I am not a swallow! I won't leave . . . not for years and years and years, maybe never. I'll breed the best horses on the plains, proud, high-stepping white horses, and get you a golden coach and a velvet gown heavy with gold and diamonds and rubies. You will look like a queen and I will take you riding all over the plains, into the towns and cities, and everywhere people will stop and look and ask: 'Who is this beautiful queen?' and I will crack my whip and shout: 'She is my mother!' "

Suddenly he lost his dreamy expression and glared at Kate. "Hey! What are you pinching me for?"

"You forgot something," said Kate demurely.

"What?"

"Us," grinned Kate. "Me and Daddy and Uncle Márton."

"No, I didn't, either. They were there all along and so were

you until you pinched me. But I guess we had better leave you home. With your chickens."

"That's all right with me," declared Kate calmly. "I like it here. I can raise thousands of chickens so they'll lay millions and millions of eggs, and I'll sell them and when I have enough money I'll buy one of those American tractors for Uncle Márton and an automobile for Daddy so he can come home every day. So there!"

"Not for me," the two brothers protested together. Márton Nagy smiled understandingly at his brother as he went on: "I'll disown you, Kate, if you even speak of those noisy, smelly, roaring brutes!"

"They go faster than Jancsi's old white horses!" pouted Kate.

"Let them. I want to walk slowly behind the plow; I want to have time to feel the soft, crumbling soil under my feet, to smell its rich, moist smell. I want to have time to look at the flowers by the fence, the blue sky above, to listen to the birds and the song of the wind. I don't want a machine puffing black smoke into God's clean air, crushing birds' nests under its cold steel claws, roaring 'Hurry-hurry-hurry' into my ears. When day is done, I want to be able to say: 'Well done, old friend,' to my horse, rub him clean, feed him sweet-smelling hay, golden oats, and fresh water. At night I want to breathe the clean air of the plains and hear the small noises contented animals make, instead of smelling stale oil and listening to the dead silence of stilled machinery."

"I feel the same way, Brother," mused Uncle Sándor, "and yet machinery will come to the plains, sooner or later."

"I know," nodded Jancsi's father. "But I also know our people. Before they give up their peaceful, unhurried ways, their very souls will have to be changed. And what could change that?"

"A war could."

"Yes. A war could destroy their dignity, their good nature, their contentment. But this is 1914, Brother. Two generations have grown up in peace; got used to thinking of people in other countries as brothers, not enemies. What would anybody start a war for? Why, our men would just laugh and go back to their plowing!"

Sándor Nagy opened his mouth as if to answer. But, looking around the old kitchen aglow with candlelight, so warm, so peaceful, he only said with a sigh: "God grant that you are right, Brother. And now"—he stretched, suppressing a yawn—"how about going to bed?"

 CHAPTER III

THE YOUNG MASTER

WHEN Sándor Nagy awoke next morning, it was still dark. For a moment he thought he had been dreaming, but then he felt a small, cold hand on his face again and heard Kate's urgent voice: "Daddy! Get up, Daddy!"

He sat up with a start. "What . . . what happened?"

"Get up, Daddy. It's late."

"But, good heavens, child, it's pitch-dark . . . the middle of the night!"

"Middle of the night nothing! It's almost four o'clock and breakfast will be ready in a minute."

51

"Don't want any. I'm on my vacation," he grumbled, turning to the wall. Swift footsteps pattered across the floor, there was the creak of a door, then Kate began again: "Dad-dyyy. Smell!"

"Go away, you imp," he groaned. Suddenly he lifted his head and sniffed the air. "What's that I smell?"

"Oh, nothing much. Just fresh bread and sausages. You don't want any."

"Oh, no? Well, you just run along, young lady, and heap up my plate to the brim."

Kate disappeared, laughing, through the open kitchen door. In a few minutes he stumbled after her, still tugging at his boot-straps. Mother was just placing a whole steaming ham on the table.

"And ham! *And* boiled eggs. . . . Here, give me a slice!" he cried, reaching for the knife. Mother snatched it away. "You go and scrub your face, Sándor," she said severely, but her eyes were twinkling.

"Don't forget your teeth . . . and behind your ears!" shouted Kate as he hurried out toward the well in the yard.

His face was scrubbed shiny and his hair was still dripping wet when he reappeared in the kitchen. Jancsi had brought in the fresh milk, then Father came in, wiping his hands on a towel.

"I've saddled three horses. Thought you might want to come along, Sándor," he said as they were sitting down to the meal. Jancsi looked at him. "How about Kate? Isn't she coming to see my herd?"

"No." Kate shook her head. "Auntie and I have a lot of sewing and ironing to do. Look"—she pointed to a basketful of white, embroidered ruffles—"all those have to go on my new petticoats."

Jancsi's fork paused between the plate and his stricken face. "Petticoats! Ruffles! I knew it, I just knew it! It all started with those red satin ribbons."

"What *are* you talking about?" smiled Mother.

"Why, she is turning into nothing but a *girl*. Aw, Kate, honest, you used to be almost as good as a boy . . . and now you don't even want to see my herd. You . . . you want ruffles!"

His voice, which had already begun to change and deepen, broke on an anguished squeak and Kate frowned at him. "Don't squeal like a baby pig. The colts will be there next week, but the wedding is tomorrow. And I am to wear thirteen petticoats." She turned proudly to her father. "Auntie said I'm almost as good as a grown-up."

"You'll look just plain funny, that's what I say," argued Jancsi. "All swollen out with skirts down below and skinny as a plucked chicken up here." He made an upward movement from his waist to his neck. "Grown-up girls are fat all over, like Mother. Aw . . . I don't care, anyway; go ahead and look funny."

Mother took a look at Kate's flashing eyes and said quickly: "She is as good as grown up when it comes to helping me! And, Jancsi, she can't stay a tomboy forever; it just isn't seemly for a big girl to go riding astride a horse!"

Now both children set up a wail. Jancsi wanted to know

how else anyone could ride but astride, and when Kate's father explained that there is such a thing as a side-saddle for ladies, even Father protested.

"Not for a self-respecting plains horse. If Mother says Kate is too old to ride like a boy, she'll just stay on the ground, but I won't have a good riding horse ruined—least of all Milky."

Milky was Kate's white horse; nobody else was allowed to ride on Milky. Tears sprang into Kate's eyes. "Oh, Auntie!"

"There, there, my lamb, don't cry. We'll make it easy for you to grow up. Look"—she pointed to the window, golden with the rising sun—"it's daylight. Take your father to see the egg factory while I wash the dishes."

But Kate was crying in earnest now. Milky was her pride and joy; she loved to ride, to roam the plains with Jancsi, he on black Bársony, she on snow-white Milky, racing, trotting, jumping fences together . . . and now all this was threatened by some strange process called "growing up." Suddenly all the coveted privileges of older girls—ruffles, thirteen petti-coats, dancing with big boys—dwindled to nothing compared to the joy of racing Jancsi across the plains into the rising sun, wind tearing at her hair, the smooth, powerful motion of her horse flowing through her body, and Jancsi's breathless praise: "You sure can ride!"

All this burst out of her in one protesting wail: "I don't want to grow up!"

"Now see what you have done!" Mother, on the verge of tears herself because she knew that there was no medicine against growing up, turned on her husband and son. "You have made her cry!"

"I?" gasped Jancsi, utterly bewildered. Father laughed. "Come on, Son, before Mother takes a broom to us. From now on this is strictly woman's business. Coming, Sándor?"

Sándor Nagy looked at Mother inquiringly. She, holding Kate with one arm, frowned and made a "go away" motion with the other. The three men, snatching up what breakfast they could rescue, went out.

At the stable Jancsi paused, with one foot in the stirrup. "Father, what *is* wrong with Kate? She never used to be this way. And what have *we* done?"

Father scratched his head. "Son, I don't know."

Uncle Sándor smiled. "Kate is changing from a tomboy child to a real girl, whether we like it or not. Growing up, as your mother said, Jancsi. She knows how hard that is because she is a woman. We don't. We are little boys one day, then suddenly we are men. Like you."

Jancsi's chest swelled but he didn't say anything for a while. They rode out of the yard and turned north on the path to the corrals. Only when they were well on the way did Jancsi break the silence.

"I know how it is. Like a butterfly."

"What's like a butterfly?" asked Father, puzzled at this unexpected statement.

"Girls. You know, Father, first there is only a grub, then an ugly little cocoon. Then, something inside begins to move and fight through and little by little a butterfly crawls out. It must be hard for the butterfly because it's always shaking and shivering, but after a while it opens its wings and flies

into the sunshine and then it looks happy . . . and . . . beautiful!
I guess . . . Kate is just . . . fighting through," he concluded,
then blushed violently when he noticed that both men were
looking at him with an odd little smile. He dug his heels into
Bársony's sides, and when the horse leaped ahead he shouted
over his shoulder:

"Last man at the ferry is a puppydog's tail!"

Uncle Sándor was the "puppydog's tail," arriving disheveled, hot, and panting at the ferry. He soon gave up even pretending to help pull the cable-drawn ferry across the river, and
just sat propped against the railing. "I am soft," he admitted
ruefully, watching his brother and nephew pull on the cables
as if they had not been riding long miles.

He was more than soft when they arrived at the corrals. He
was sore and very unsteady on his feet. Jancsi laughed at him
as he stood clinging to his horse for support.

"Now you look just like Kate did after her first riding
lesson. Funny face and all!"

"Ugh!" he grunted, taking a few wavering steps. " 'And
all' doesn't feel so funny. It hurts!"

"Saddlesore, Mr. Nagy?" smiled Old Arpád who had ridden
up to greet them. "You will soon harden up again. Used to be
quite a rider when you were a young one like Jancsi here. But,"
he sighed, "that was a long time ago. I have grown old and
he has grown up to be our young master."

If somebody had handed the Hungarian plains to Jancsi on
a silver platter, he could not have felt what he was feeling
now. The young master! Old Arpád had called him that! His

father was known far and wide as the Good Master and now
. . . Some unknown, strong, and heady feeling was swelling
in Jancsi's heart, making it beat wildly against his chest, choking him until he almost gasped. The young master! "I will
be . . . I *will* be . . . like Father!" he thought, and his fists
clenched with his effort to keep from crying. "I will be." It
was a prayer and a promise to himself and to his father, the
first conscious resolution of boy growing into man.

He didn't speak, only stood there, oblivious of the three
men looking at him, but the flush on his face, the straightening
of his shoulders, and the shining light in his eyes must have
told his father something. Jancsi felt his strong hand on his
shoulder and heard his voice, proud, strong and yet gentle,
saying the words he should have said: "Thank you, Old Arpád.
With your help, he will be."

"Yes, sir." The storm burst out of Jancsi in a shout and he
was boy again, burning with impatience. "Where is my herd?"

"Still in the corrals—the boys are building a fence for them
in the south pasture," smiled Old Arpád.

Jancsi was already racing toward the large triangular en-
closure divided into corrals. In one of them he saw what he
was looking for and yelled:

"Here they are! Hurry up. *Look* at them!"

He was inside, his arms around two long-legged little colts,
when the men arrived at the gate. "Colts, Father, the twins!
What a team they will make! Shining chestnuts with white
stars on their foreheads . . . just look! And one black . . . there,
by the black mare." He whirled about, sending the tiny twins

into awkward prancing with a slap on their little rumps. "And I told you, I told you, I *told* you the pinto would have a white foal!" He pointed to another mare, nursing her small, questionably white offspring.

"He did too, Mr. Nagy," murmured Old Arpád to Uncle Sándor, "and we laughed at him. And he was right, the little tyke was right!"

They walked away toward the house, leaving Jancsi with his animals. The young herders were just riding in for their lunch.

"I bet they don't know what it is to be saddlesore," sighed Sándor Nagy as he watched these bronzed, sturdy men of the plains. Horse and man seemed to be all of a piece, moving together in perfect harmony. They dismounted at the house and went inside for their meal—all but one. He stayed on his horse, waiting. In a few moments Old Arpád's wife came out and gave him his meal, which he proceeded to eat in the saddle.

"The young idiot!" chuckled Old Arpád, shaking his head.

"Hey, Pali, can't you walk?" shouted Jancsi's father. The young herder doffed his hat, grinned sheepishly, but didn't answer. Old Arpád, still laughing, turned to Father. "He swore that he will not set foot on the ground—except to sleep —for six months."

"But why?"

"You know, Mr. Nagy, that he had been away for his Army service." Father nodded. "And," said Old Arpád shaking with laughter, "those boneheads at the recruiting office kept him—a herder, a man who lives on his horse!—in the infantry for three years! He came back here last night, footsore and as mad as a wet hen, swearing that he won't walk another step for six months! And, by everything that's holy, he means it!"

"Can you blame him?" chuckled Father.

"I can't even blame him for the things he says about the Army. We didn't teach him the language he uses now; they did. You could fry an egg on some of the words he has learned."

Jancsi had come up too and was listening with both ears. "Let's go and talk to him," he proposed hopefully.

"I'd like to, myself," said Uncle Sándor.

"Well, Pali," Father smiled at the young herder, "I hear you didn't care for Army life."

"Mind your words now!" warned Old Arpád. Pali minded them. His face got red and redder in the effort, but his tongue didn't slip.

"Mr. Nagy," he began, "three years they have kept me away from home, the plains, my horse. For what? To climb up and down those almighty high mountains they grow in the north, to lie on my stomach in the black mud down south and shoot guns at nothing. To peel potatoes, polish brass buttons, wash dishes like a woman, make beds so neat and tight that a flea would scream if it tried to get under the covers. To march, march, march all day, carrying blankets, overcoat, gun, bayonet, ammunition, food, water, bandages—all day, mind you, just to tote them home again at night. To eat bread and water in solitary . . ." He blushed a still deeper red and stopped.

"What for? Out with it!" laughed Father.

Pali shrugged. "For . . . well, for trying to help the top sergeant."

"They wouldn't lock you up for that!" cried Jancsi.

"That one did. He was an Austrian, like the rest of them, and the poor fish can't speak like decent folks. All day he had been hollering at us until he had no voice left and his poor eyes were popping. So I stepped out of line and told him"—an amused smile twitched Pali's perky little mustache, and he pushed his hat way back on his head—"told him good and loud that if he'd stop braying like a homeless jackass, we would know what he wanted."

The men burst out laughing. "You, a rookie, told *that* to a top sergeant?" gasped Father.

"Sure, and why not? It was God's own truth," grinned Pali. "But he just got madder than he was before and made the whole company march into the swamps. When we were knee-deep in water and mud he yelled: 'Down!' and down we went, on our stomachs. 'Do *that* a hundred times,' he bawled, 'and next time you'll understand me, you.' . . . Oh, well there was something more. Anyway, I stood it for a few times, but then I got to thinking about all the buttons we'd have to polish, so I got mad too and I went up to him and pushed his grinning face where the mud was softest. So, they locked me up."

"No wonder. You have to obey orders when you are in the Army. That's why everybody has to serve; to learn discipline," said Sándor Nagy, half laughing, half serious. Pali turned his intent, sincere gaze at him. "Orders, Mr. Nagy? I have learned to obey orders from Old Arpád. If he as much as lifts an eyebrow, I'll break my neck to do what he wants. Nobody has to roar at me like that braying jackass to make me do my job."

"Soldiering was your job for three years, Pali," said Uncle Sándor. Father spoke too: "All of us have to do our Army service; it's the law."

"And a very foolish law it is, Mr. Nagy," said Old Arpád, shaking his head. "Pushing guns into young men's hands instead of giving them tools to use or their own jobs to do. Making them play war when our worst enemy is the locust and the horsefly. Teaching them to crawl on their stomachs before a make-believe enemy, now, Mr. Nagy, what is the sense in that? If there is an enemy to fight, give a man a horse and a saber and he will show you how men fight if they have to: like men, not worms!" He lowered his voice and frowned. "The Austrians have made those laws, Mr. Nagy. An Austrian is wearing the holy crown of Saint Stephen. They have chained the Eagle of Attila to the two-headed eagle of the Habsburgs. Will it always be so, Mr. Nagy? Always?"

Sándor Nagy held up his hand. "Old Arpád, Hungary formed an alliance with Austria almost two hundred years ago. Since then, many things have threatened this alliance, discontent on both sides, revolutions, wars. But the Empire has survived, grown strong and prosperous. The Emperor is our King and *because* he is wearing the crown of Saint Stephen, we must respect his laws. We have given our word, and by our word we must abide." He smiled at Old Arpád. "Thus speaks the schoolmaster, old friend. Sándor Nagy adds: Whether we like them or not."

Pali leaned down from his horse. "They don't like us, Mr. Nagy. I didn't like to say it, but that braying jackass of an Austrian called us, begging your pardon, he called us Magyar dogs. And the rookies who came from down south, he called them Serb pigs. The little mild Slovaks from the mountains were smelly goats to him."

Sándor Nagy interrupted. "He must have been a very stupid man, Pali; they aren't all like that."

Pali straightened up again and his eyes flashed. "No, Mr. Nagy, they don't like us. I heard a lot of talk in those three years. I got so I could understand German. And when I was on duty at the officers' mess, I heard a lot of talk. One of them, a general he was, said that their day will soon come. The old Emperor will die, he said, and then, then Francis Ferdinand will show the Magyar and Slavish rabble what an iron fist means. He laughed when he said that, the way a wolf laughs with all his teeth asnarl, and it's lucky for him I was at the other end of the messhall or I would have dumped the soup tureen on his bald head . . . so help me!"

"Lucky for *you*, I should say," sighed Sándor Nagy. He didn't laugh at Pali's expressive gesture of dumping soup on a general's bald head. His eyes were troubled as he looked at his brother, then at Old Arpád and at Jancsi. He saw indignation and deeply hurt pride in each of these beloved faces. Something inside him turned cold as if an icy hand had touched his heart, and for a moment he thought he heard the far-off rumble of thunder. But the sky was an unbroken deep blue; there was only one tiny puff of cloud on the horizon. "A small thing like that could not mean a storm," he thought irrelevantly. Then he shook his head as if to shake off some vague fear; he became aware of the others again, of the question in their eyes.

"Forget it, Pali!" he cried, trying to sound cheerful. "It was only talk. The old Emperor is hale and well; Francis Ferdinand might die before him. Forget it. There won't be any war."

He heard his own words as if someone else had spoken them and drew in his breath sharply, but it was too late. Old Arpád laid a hand on his shoulder and said slowly, kindly: "Who said anything about war, Mr. Nagy?"

"I did. Stupid of me," said Sándor Nagy almost gruffly. Then he smiled. "Schoolteachers always talk too much, especially when they are hungry. And this one is very hungry."

"That is my fault," smiled Old Arpád. "Here I stand gossiping like womenfolk instead of offering you a meal. If you will honor my table . . ." He stood aside, waiting for them to go inside. His words were humble but his gesture was that of a king. So was the one level glance he gave the loitering herders. In a moment they were in their saddles, riding off, back to the herds. Only Pali lagged behind, his eyes still on Uncle Sándor.

"Pali," said Old Arpád in the gentlest voice. Pali wheeled his horse and galloped away.

"Army discipline almost ruined that boy," chuckled Old Arpád, following his guests to the table.

 CHAPTER IV

THE WEDDING

SUNDAY began like any other day on the ranch. The family was up with the first crow of the roosters and when the sun pushed its round, red face over the horizon, they were almost through with the morning meal.

Father, Jancsi, and Uncle Sándor were talking placidly about some fences and new buildings; Mother, waiting for them to rise from the table, sat stitching, equally placidly, on a piece of embroidery. Kate, who had rushed through her morning chores and gulped down her breakfast, began to squirm in her chair. Nobody paid any attention to her. She

67

twisted and fidgeted, sat forward and pushed back again, made little noises in her throat as if she had a cold, until Mother looked up from her embroidery. Seeing the anxious expression on Kate's face, she gave her a little nod and said soundlessly: "You may go."

Kate shook her head impatiently. "No, Auntie, no."

"What is it, then?"

"The wedding! Aren't we going to get dressed for the wedding?" whispered Kate.

"I should say not," said Mother.

"Auntie! Aren't we ... aren't we going?" This was a wail, loud enough to make the men look up and take notice.

"Of course we are going. But we can't get dressed until we have been called. It would not be seemly," explained Mother calmly.

"Called? You mean invited? But we *have* been invited. Everybody has been invited. Why ... why, Auntie! The dresses and food we got ready! . . ." stammered Kate. Still Mother didn't move. "We haven't been called yet," was all she said.

"Daddy!" Kate appealed to her father. "I just don't understand."

"You will in a little while." He smiled. "You will see an ancient ceremony, the 'wedding call.' The words and formalities in that ceremony are almost as old as the Magyar race. Every word the callers will say, every word your uncle will say, has been said in just that way at every Hungarian wedding for hundreds of years. It's a tradition we would not dare change."

"They should be here any minute now," said Jancsi.

"Yes, and we had better get to work. It won't do at all to let them find us waiting," said Father, rising from the table.

To Kate's consternation, everybody got very busy—chopping wood, although there was a huge pile already chopped; brushing horses, although they shone like satin anyway; carrying water to the kitchen, although the pails were full with the daily supply. Mother insisted that Kate help her with the dishes, a task she usually didn't want any help with. After the last dish had been polished, she said:

"Open the windows in the 'clean' room, Kate, and dust the chairs." The "clean" room was very seldom opened. It was a kind of parlor reserved for the most festive occasions and kept dark most of the time but always scrupulously clean. Any visitor who was led into the clean room was an honored guest indeed. Kate's puzzled question: "Why, Auntie, who in the world is coming?" went unanswered because Mother cried: "Hurry! Here they come."

Opening the windows and shutters of the clean room, Kate saw two wagons drive into the yard. And what wagons! They had been freshly painted and each was pulled by four white horses. Wagons and horses were all but covered with wreaths of flowers and ribbons; there were flowers tied to the whips of the drivers, to the headbands of the horses, to the whiffletrees and the wheels. Men, young and old, came piling off, dressed in the gayest of their always gay and colorful holiday costumes. The wide sleeves of their shirts and their pleated, full trousers were dazzlingly white, their vests were a colorful riot of appliqué work and embroidery, their boots were so glossy that—an impish thought came into Kate's head and she giggled —"a fly would break its neck on them." And the hats! High and black, they were wound around and around with many colored ribbons, encircled with flowers.

Father was walking toward them, followed by his brother and Jancsi. The men stood in an orderly line and one of them, evidently their leader because he carried a flower-laden staff, stepped forward.

"Kate!" called Mother from the doorway. "Come quickly, the 'call' is beginning." She and Kate hurried out just when Father began to speak.

"May the Lord give a good day to all you men. What happy event has brought you such a long way to our modest home?"

"A very good day to you, our host," spoke the leader. "It is a great honor for us to be received in your good home."

Father stepped aside, indicating the door with an out-stretched arm. "Please enter and accept our hospitality."

"We thank you," said the leader. Slowly they walked in, through the kitchen, into the clean room, followed by the family. There the men stood in a line again, the leader stepped forward, and knocked with his staff on the floor.

"Our kind host," he began, "we have come to ask for your help and the help of all your dear family."

"We are at your service," said Father seriously.

"We are," repeated Mother, Jancsi, and Kate's father. Kate, to whom all this was like a play, piped up a moment later: "Me, too."

"Thank you." The leader bowed his head, then went on: "There is a little white dove back home where we came from; a little white dove, pure and gentle. She has been kept in a cage all her life, but this spring the door of her cage has been opened. She has flown off to the woods and there heard the call of her mate."

"That is as it should be," Father said.

"That is as it should be," nodded the leader. "Now, the little white dove and her mate are ready to build their nest. We, who have known her all her life and know she is deserving, have come to ask you, dear host, to help feather her nest."

"We will," said Father.

The leader lifted his staff high, then knocked with it on the floor three times. "And so we call you to the wedding of the maid Mari Vidor and the lad Peter Hódi, to the feast and the rejoicing at the house of János Vidor, and to the 'Lead Me Home' procession tonight." He paused for a moment, then added: "You have been called."

"We have been called," said Father, "and we shall come gladly."

With Father's last words the ceremony was over. The men relaxed, began to move around and talk about everyday things. Father and Mother brought in bread and wine and invited the callers to sit down. This, however was politely declined; they each took a bite of bread and a sip of wine, then shook hands with everybody and left.

The moment the wagons turned down the lane, Mother closed the windows and shutters of the clean room. "Now hurry, all of you, and get dressed!" she cried. "I don't want to be late for the wedding. Hurry!"

"Auntie," mumbled Kate, struggling into her petticoats, "why couldn't we have dressed before? We knew we were going!"

"It would have seemed forward to take it for granted. We ... they ... oh, don't ask me questions now, Kate. Help me lace this bodice." Mother gasped. "Good gracious, how these materials shrink!"

Kate pulled at the laces with all her might. "There! You look fine, Auntie—just as if you had been poured into it. Not a wrinkle!"

"I feel like a stuffed goose," sighed Mother, "but that can't be helped. Let me see you now. Bonnet, blouse, bodice, petticoats,. skirt, apron, boots . . . yes, you'll do. Get the prayerbooks and the lace kerchiefs. Don't wrinkle them, now! Here we go."

"How these doors shrink!" giggled Kate when Mother, in her innumerable petticoats, pleated skirt, and apron, had to be pushed and coaxed through the narrow door. Suddenly Mother let out a little shriek and stood still. "What is it, Auntie?" cried Kate, trying to peek around the considerable girth of her aunt. "Oh, my holy Saints! Jancsi!"

They both gaped at the strangely tall and broad-shouldered young man who, a little while ago, was just plain Jancsi. He stood between his father and uncle, almost as tall as they were; perhaps he was standing on tiptoe . . . but he had good reasons for it. For the first time in his life he was dressed as only the big ranchers are dressed on the plains; exactly like Father, tight-fitting blue coat with braids on, slim blue riding-breeches, patent-leather boots—even a soft silk tie.

"Mother, meet the young master—Jancsi, in case you don't know him," said Father putting his arm around Jancsi's shoulder. "I was rather surprised myself," he added with a smile.

Kate found her voice first. "Why, Jancsi, it's perfectly bee-eautiful!" she cried, running around him in circles.

"Aw, go on! A man can't be beautiful," grumbled Jancsi, not at all displeased.

"You aren't so bad yourself, at that." But his eyes were on Mother, who still hadn't spoken. Now she smiled and said:

"It's fine, Jancsi, fine. Only you look so much the way your Father used to when I first met him . . . it gave me quite a turn."

"Do I?" cried Jancsi, pulling himself still straighter if possible. "Well, then that's all right! Let's go!"

The men eased Mother and Kate into the wagon, carefully, as if they were baskets of eggs. Uncle Sándor sat between them, all but covered with the overflowing ruffles, ribbons, and laces.

"Want to drive, Son?" asked Father.

"No, sir. I am riding Bársony," declared Jancsi.

"You are? Who said so?" frowned Father.

"I am saying so. If we are going to stay for the 'Lead Me Home,' we won't be back until late. Somebody has got to milk the cows because . . ."

"A cow isn't interested in excuses. All a cow wants is to be milked!" chanted the whole family, laughing at Father's surprised face.

"And that is my job," declared Jancsi sturdily. "I'll ride home at sundown and be back for the 'Lead Me Home.' You go on; I'll catch up with you," he cried, running toward the stable.

"And that, dear Brother," laughed Uncle Sándor, "sounds like an order from the boss."

Father pulled his hat over his eyes with an almost boyish gesture. "That *was* an order, or I don't know the voice of authority. What a boy!"

He swung himself into the seat. "Come up here, Sándor. You look like a June bug drowned in whipped cream back there."

"Besides," he whispered to his brother when the wagon was on its way, "it would be kind of lonesome up here . . . alone."

Jancsi, riding Bársony, caught up with them at the end of the lane. Once on the main road, they became part of the long line of wagons, carriages, and riders, all headed for the village. People were singing, shouting to one another and to the Nagys. One wagon carried a whole gypsy band, playing lively tunes. The sun was laughing down at the plains from a cloudless blue sky and the plains seemed to be laughing back in a burst of brilliant color and gay song.

By the time Father found a place for the wagon and horses, the small church was packed to overflowing. So, to Mother's disappointment, they had to stand on the steps. Behind them the crowd grew and grew, until people completely filled the square. From the sound of murmuring voices broken by moments of stillness and the ringing of the acolytes' bells inside the church, they could follow the service. They all joined in the singing of hymns and, when the organ rang out triumphantly, pronouncing the end of the ceremony, the singing and shouting, mingled with the booming bells in the steeple, must have reached the gates of Heaven and made the angels smile.

There was a stir in the wide doorway of the church, the crowd parted, and the bridal procession began to move slowly down the steps. The bride Mari Vidor, dressed in foaming, glistening white, seemed to float on the crest of a wave, a wave of color. She was surrounded by her bridesmaids and, as soon as she reached the lowest step, was whisked off, back to her father's house. The girls and women scattered into groups, each group taking up its post in a different house along the main street. The men and boys stayed with Peter and began the traditional game, the "Seeking." Led by the "callers" and followed by the softly playing gypsies, they went from house to house. At every door they stopped and Peter knocked.

"Good people in this house, I have lost my white dove, my white dove has flown away. Help me find her, good people."

The door was opened and the women, who had arrived there only a short while before, came out.

"We have not seen your white dove, but help you we will."

This was repeated over and over again and the procession grew. The whole village was behind Peter when finally they reached the Vidor farm. Here Peter repeated his call and Mari's mother opened the door.

"I have seen your white dove, and find her you will," she said. A great shouting and cheering broke out at these words and the gypsies crashed into a wild tune. The crowd formed a large half-circle around the door. János Vidor appeared, leading a bent old woman by the hand. "May this be the white dove you are seeking?"

Peter walked around the old woman solemnly. Then he stepped back and shook his head. "This one is too old to be my white dove.

Now Mari's mother came, leading a small girl. "May this be the white dove you are seeking?"

Again Peter shook his head. "This one is too young to be my white dove."

One by one they led out tall girls, short girls, fat girls, thin girls, but to each one Peter objected, to the immense amusement of the crowd. The game went on and on, the hilarity grew. Then, suddenly the bride appeared in the doorway and everybody shouted: "May this be the white dove you are seeking?"

Peter threw his hat into the air and cried: "This is my white dove I have been seeking!"

The crowd cheered, the band swung into a csárdás, and Peter swept Mari into the dance. This was the sign for the real festivities to begin. Young and old danced, faster and faster, the bride flew from hand to hand, around and around, until she had danced with every man. Then she was led back

to Peter, who had danced with every girl and woman. Together they led the cheering guests back of the house to the garden and orchard, where long, sturdy tables had been piled high with food and drinks. The food visible on the tables was only a beginning; more came every minute, brought from the wagons of the guests and the neighbors' kitchens. There were roast pigs and lambs, chickens, geese, and ducks by the dozens, mountains of sausages, hams, pastries, cakes, baskets of bread, buns, and rolls.

Kate, disheveled and hot but happy, saw Jancsi take possession of a whole chicken and a plate of cakes. He was making his way toward the little brook at the foot of the orchard. Kate ran after him. "Here, give me some. Isn't this wonderful?" she cried, relieving him of the plate. He gave her an unhappy glance. "Yes? Look what's waiting for you." Kate followed the derisive jerk of his chin and groaned:

"Oh, my good saints! Where did she come from?"

Leaning very affectedly against a tree stood Lily. That Lily! She was twirling a lace parasol over her shoulder and surveyed the gay scene around her with a haughty expression.

"What does she think she is, a plaster saint?" scoffed Kate, plopping a whole tart into her mouth. "Well, you found it, Jancsi, you keep it," she grinned. "I am going. . . ."

It was too late. Lily was waving a white-gloved hand.

"You see?" muttered Jancsi. "She'll stick like a bur and ruin our whole day."

"Not while I am around," whispered Kate with such conviction that Jancsi looked at her suspiciously.

"What are you going to do?"

Kate shrugged. "Something will happen. Don't know what yet. Hello, Lily!" she added with deceptive cordiality.

"Oh, Kate dear," piped Lily, "isn't this frightful? The smell and heat and this . . . uncouth crowd! I feel faint already!"

"Maybe you are hungry. Here, have a leg," offered Jancsi, tearing off a chicken leg and holding it out to her. She made a face. "Ugh! It makes me ill to look at that food."

"Why don't you go home, then?" asked Jancsi, taking a huge bite of the chicken.

"I can't. Father insisted that we stay. He has to keep friendly with the peasants, he said. He made me come home for my vacation too . . . and I could have gone to the Riviera with such delightful friends!"

"To where?" asked Jancsi.

"The Riviera, a French watering place, you know."

"Oh. We have a watering place here, down by the cattle-run. I could take you wading if you want me to," said Jancsi. "Not in that nightshirt, though; you'll have to wear something shorter," he added, indicating Lily's long, draped gown.

"Cattlerun . . . nightshirt . . ." squeaked Lily. "I want you to know that this is a Paris model, you silly little boy. And the French Riviera isn't a wading place! Why, it's elegant. People parade up and down all day long on the seashore and every night they dance in the most marvelous hotels and . . ."

"Huh. You can dance all you want to here," grunted Jancsi, not at all impressed. "Look, Kate, they're beginning to dance again and look! There is Uncle Moses and Aunt Sarah . . . there, with Father. Don't they look nice? Uncle Moses!" he hollered, waving a chicken leg at the old couple. They were coming slowly across the orchard, clinging to the arms of Father, watching the dance with an almost childish enjoyment in their kind old faces.

Lily sniffed. "Really, Kate, this is too much. A man like your uncle associating with . . ."

Kate spun around, her eyes flashing fire, ready to pour all her resentment into a sharp answer. But there was no time for anything now because happy, boisterous Peter had sprung out of the thick of dancing couples and grabbed Lily around the waist.

"One dance for good luck, Miss Lily. Play, gypsies, play for your lives!" he shouted. "Take your hands off me!" yelled Lily, pushing her hands against him. "How dare you," she went on, raising her voice, "you uncouth jackass! How dare you!"

A few couples had stopped dancing and many were looking curiously in the direction of the angry voice. Peter's brown, flushed face paled. Looking straight at Lily, he asked slowly: "How dare I what, Miss Lily? How dare I what?"

Now a little murmur, hardly more than a whisper, started up among the people. Not threatening, not even angry; it was just like the ripple of cold wind that so often was the first sign of approaching storm on the plains. Older people, sitting around the tables, were getting up, craning their necks to see what had happened; all the dancers had stopped, looking toward the now silent group.

Kate cast an anxious glance first at Peter's pale face, then all around her. She knew these people. She had seen happy gatherings like this spoiled by a careless word or gesture. Without thinking, because afterwards she could not remember having thought at all, she brought the sharp heel of her boot down on Lily's toes. Lily let out a howl that could be heard all over the orchard. "Kate . . . you . . . !"

"Uncouth jackass," supplied Kate hastily. "I'm sorry, Lily. I must have slipped. Now you can't dance with Peter," she babbled on, glancing at Peter's dumfounded face, "but maybe he'll come back later. Won't you, Peter?"

"First he will have to dance with me, though," said a small voice, and there was little Aunt Sarah, holding out her hands to Peter, smiling at him. He was still too confused to react immediately and she went on: "I really used to be a very good dancer when I was young"—she smiled at Uncle Moses— "wasn't I, Papa?"

Now all Peter's native courtesy was aroused. "Young! You will always be young, Aunt Sarah!" he cried. "We will show them what good dancing is."

He held up his hands. "Men, take your partners out to the clearing. Gypsies, play the kör-magyar! Mr. Nagy"—he turned to Father—"will you be our leader?"

"Gladly, Peter, gladly," said Father heartily. "Even if my best girl deserted me for you." He smiled, patting Aunt Sarah's hand. "Take care of her now!"

Peter threw his arms around the old lady. "I'll treat her like a basket of peacock eggs, Mr. Nagy, don't you worry."

They lined up for the kör-magyar, a many-figured ancient group dance of the Hungarian countryside. Jancsi, with suppressed amusement on his face, asked Kate to dance it with him but she shook her head and said in a voice almost dripping with honey: "I will just take care of pooooor Lily."

Jancsi turned away hastily to hide the grin he could no longer conceal. "Did you see that angel-face on Kate?" he whispered to Uncle Moses as they walked toward the dancers, "Heaven help pooooor Lily now!"

Uncle Moses peered at him sideways and if dignified old men wink at all, he certainly did. "With Kate for a go-between, Heaven will no doubt help Lily to what she deserves."

Kate and Lily were left alone under the apple tree. Lily was still nursing her bruised toes, blubbering and sniffling, for, after all, she was only thirteen years old.

"You . . . you did that on purpose!" She glared at Kate now. "You ruined my slippers . . . on purpose."

Kate didn't answer. She was kneeling in front of Lily, looking straight at her, but she didn't seem to hear the peevish voice. If only she could find some means of getting Lily out of the way before she started some serious trouble. But how?

"Why don't you say something?" whined Lily. "I said you did it on purpose. You were jealous because Peter wanted to dance with *me*, that's why!"

"What?" Kate seemed to come out of a dream. "Oh, Lily, I was thinking. You might get . . . blood-poisoning or something. Hadn't we better go home and put a hot poultice on your foot?"

"No."

"Auntie always puts a hot poultice on my foot when a horse steps on it."

"No."

"Well . . . maybe it's . . . broken," said Kate, trying not to sound hopeful. This was a mistake. Lily, forgetting all her airs, started to howl "I want a doctor!"

"Oh, now, Lily . . . maybe it isn't broken. We can tell. Try to stand on it. Come on, get up. If you can stand on it, then it isn't broken. There . . . it's all right." She sighed as Lily stood on both feet. "Now we'll go home and put a hot poultice on it."

"We got iodine home to put on. Hot poultice is a stupid peasant remedy," sniffed Lily, hobbling along. Kate swallowed even this, as long as Lily was going.

"All right. We'll put anything on it you say, and then I'll put you to bed."

"No. I'm coming right back and tell that Peter what I think of him . . . mauling a lady!" She stopped. "I'll tell him right now. My foot is all right, let me go!"

But Kate didn't let go. She was holding on to Lily for dear life. They were alone in the back alley leading from one farm to the other, among chicken-coops, pigsties, and small barns. Except for the animals, all the farms were deserted; everybody had gone to the dance.

"Let me go!" gasped Lily, trying to pull away. Kate was losing her patience fast. Seizing Lily's arm very firmly, she said: "You are going home."

"I won't" squealed Lily, grasping the post of an open barn door. "Let me go! Help! Father, heeeelp!" she screamed as Kate tried, none too gently, to pry her loose.

"Well, if you won't, you won't," sighed Kate, releasing her suddenly, and just as suddenly she pushed the surprised girl inside the barn. Lily stumbled and sprawled into a pile of straw, screeching at the top of her voice. The next moment the door banged and she heard the heavy bar drop into place. She was locked in.

Outside, Kate stood leaning against the door, still angry, listening to the rumpus Lily was raising inside. She screamed and howled, she banged at the door and kicked it. Any other time a noise like this would have been heard all over the village but not today, not with the band playing and every soul at the dance. It would be hours before anyone came near the barn, thought Kate, and her eyes began to twinkle. Then she giggled, thinking what those white gloves and silk dress would look like by that time. The fine lace parasol lay on the grass where Lily had dropped it. Kate picked it up, sent a silent grin toward the shaking barn door, and marched off.

On the Vidor farm the kör-magyar was still going on. Thus far nobody had missed her. Hiding the parasol under her apron, she was edging from tree to tree when she saw Jancsi detach himself from the crowd and wave to her. They met behind an old apple tree, hiding like conspirators. Kate held up the parasol and grinned at Jancsi.

"What did you do with the rest?" asked Jancsi, returning the grin.

"She's locked in Váradi's barn, yelling her head off," replied Kate in a matter-of-fact way. "Look, Jancsi," she went on, opening the parasol, "if I propped this up behind the tree like this, would you think Lily was behind it?"

Jancsi stepped back and gave the parasol a critical glance. "I might, if I didn't know better."

"Well, then, that's where she is." Kate sighed. She dusted her hands like someone who has finished a hard job, straightened her bonnet, and winked at Jancsi. "I'm hungry. Come on, let's eat."

Eat and dance, dance and eat; that's what everybody did all afternoon. Holidays like this were few and far between for these hardworking people, but when one came they threw themselves into the gaiety with the complete abandon of children. This time more than ever. It had been a good spring, crops showed all the promise of a good harvest; no one had cause to worry. God had sent them His blessings in sunshine, in good health, and they expressed their thankfulness the only way they could: in song, music, and happy laughter.

Late in the afternoon the tired gypsies were given a rest. People separated into groups, talking, singing, playing games. Some of the men were going home to tend their animals before dark so they could take part in the "Lead Me Home" procession. Jancsi, before he left, fished Kate out of a bunch of young people playing "run, sheep, run."

"Listen, Kate," he said, pulling her aside, "hadn't you better tell Father? You know, about Lily. I feel . . . sort of funny."

Kate nodded ruefully. "I've been feeling funny all afternoon but . . . do you suppose Judge Kormos will be very angry?"

Jancsi sighed. "You go and tell Father first. He saw what happened; he'll understand." He gave her an encouraging push. "Go on, tell him. I'll be back before dark."

Kate stood undecided for a few minutes. Then she swallowed, smoothed down her hair, straightened her rumpled skirts, and went in search of her uncle. She saw him after a while, sitting at a table with Uncle Moses, her own father, and, of all people, Judge Kormos. Mother and Aunt Sarah were there too, all of them absorbed in conversation. Nobody paid any attention to Kate's frantic signaling. She edged closer, trying to keep behind the Judge's back. She had almost reached Uncle Márton when Judge Kormos looked up and asked the only question Kate wasn't prepared to answer: "Kate, what became of Lily?" Kate stood as if rooted to the ground. "Oh . . . hmm . . . oh, Lily!" she gasped, jerking her head toward the spot where the open parasol shimmered like a huge toadstool. "Lily," she repeated in a very small voice, casting a desperate glance at Uncle Márton. He was smiling in a funny way. "We saw that hours ago. There's no Lily behind it. What did you do with her? Out with it."

Kate's lips began to quiver. This was awful. It would have been all right to tell him and explain why she had done away with Lily, but she couldn't even begin now, not with Judge Kormos looking at her from under his eyebrows the way he was. She couldn't tell tales on his own daughter. It never occurred to her to deny having had anything to do with Lily's absence or wonder how they knew that she had. She just plunged: "Locked her in Váradi's barn," then shut her eyes and waited for whatever was going to happen.

Nothing happened. Nobody spoke, there was only silence. Then something that sounded like a suppressed giggle made Kate open one eye. Aunt Sarah had both hands clapped against her mouth like a mischievous little girl and above her hands her eyes were sparkling. Uncle Moses chuckled, Uncle Márton and Kate's father laughed out loud, and the big round stomach of Judge Kormos began to heave. His face got very red and suddenly laughter popped out of him like water from a bursting dam.

Márton Nagy pulled his astonished niece to him. "It's all right, Kate, don't look so scared. Didn't we tell you," he turned to the Judge, "didn't we tell you to leave it to Kate?"

Judge Kormos only nodded because laughter was still rumbling out of him, but Kate found her voice. "But . . . aren't you . . . angry?"

"Angry enough to leave her where she is," sighed the Judge, wiping his eyes. He reached out and patted Kate's hand, smiling at her, then his face turned serious.

"That boarding school in the city," he said to Márton Nagy, "well, it was a mistake. But with my wife so ill . . ." He lifted his hands and let them drop in a discouraged gesture. "People have just begun to get used to me, and now Lily comes home acting like a little fool. . . . Why, I can't go around explaining to everybody that she is just a child aping those brainless, snobbish friends of hers in school. Some day she'll say something when there's no one around to step on her toes"—he smiled at Kate again—"or lock her in Váradi's barn, and then I'll have the whole village against me."

He paused, then shrugged his shoulders. "Well, friends, it's my problem, not yours. Let us enjoy the day while my 'problem' is locked up in Váradi's barn."

"We wouldn't be friends if we didn't share our problems," said Márton Nagy slowly. "We can share this one too."

Judge Kormos glanced up. "How?"

Kate felt her uncle's arm tighten about her and she looked up at him, but his eyes were on Mother's face. "We have a large house," he said, and it sounded like a question. She smiled. "And a small family. . . ."

Márton Nagy nodded. The pressure of his arm on Kate's shoulder grew stronger.

"Small but smart," he chuckled, shifting his smiling gaze to Kate's father. "The last little 'problem' we had turned out to be a blessing; why not try another one?" Now he was looking at Judge Kormos. "If you and your wife would let Lily spend the summer with us, we'd be glad to have her."

"Let Lily . . . !" exploded the Judge, his face beaming all over. "Why, Márton, I've been trying to get up enough courage to ask you to take her!" He rose and reached for his hat. "I'll go and tell my wife and have Lily's clothes packed."

"Oh." A small, discouraged note escaped Kate. Uncle Márton hugged her a little closer and laughingly shook his head. "Oh, no, you won't. Lily will dress the way we do on the farm or go without clothes."

For a moment Judge Kormos looked at him and hesitated, then he turned and walked away, laughing to himself. They watched him as he passed from group to group; everywhere he was greeted warmly. "They like him," said Kate's father. Márton Nagy nodded. "He is the best judge we have had and I want to keep him here."

Uncle Moses leaned way back on his chair and said to no one in particular: "Leave it to Kate."

Kate, who sat stunned, speechless, and far from happy at the prospect of having Lily for two months on the farm, came to life. "Uncle Moses," she wailed, "you are teasing me. I didn't know that ... this was going to happen! This is awful!"

"Oh, I don't know," said Uncle Moses. "You know, Kate, years and years ago, when my Aaron"—he interrupted himself and beamed at Father—"my lawyer son, my Aaron, he is coming home tonight, he has got his diploma. Anyway, when Aaron was a little bit of a boy, a nasty strange dog came to the village. He was ugly, he snapped at everybody, and the men were all for shooting him. To this day I don't know what made me take him in. Mama scolded me, the children were afraid of him, and I didn't really want a dog, but I fed him and he stayed with us.

"That Summer little Aaron fell into the deep pond by the mill and he would have drowned. But the strange dog whom nobody wanted pulled him out. Remember, Mama?"

Aunt Sarah took his hand. "And we called him Barát, Friend, because he was a friend. He got to be such a nice dog everybody liked him."

"You see, Kate," smiled Uncle Moses, "I didn't know, either, what was going to happen. It's strange . . . feed a stray dog, you step on somebody's toes, then things happen and you find that you are glad you did what you did."

Kate sighed. "Maybe. I wish I had stepped harder. I'd feel better now. Will she . . . will we take her tonight?"

"I don't think so," smiled Uncle Márton. "One wagon wouldn't hold the two of you tonight. But look!" he exclaimed. "They are getting ready for the procession. I'll get the wagon."

"And we will say good night now," said Uncle Moses, helping Aunt Sarah to her feet. "Aaron is coming in on the evening train; we want to be home to welcome our lawyer son. Now we've got a lawyer, a doctor, and a rabbi in the family; three smart sons to take care of us in this life . . . and the next. We have nothing to worry about any more, have we, Mama?"

Something caught in Kate's throat at the sight of the old couple, standing there in the gathering dusk, smiling at each other, so old, so bent, with their work-worn gnarled hands interlaced, so humble and yet so proud. The others must have seen them the way she did, because Mother said: "I am so glad for you," and her voice shook a little.

"So are we all," said Father warmly. "If anyone deserves a happy old age, you two certainly do. Come, I'll walk home with you."

He walked between them, tall, straight, powerful—the old couple, very tired now, leaning on his arms confidently. Here and there torches were lighted, first two, then three, then more and more, in readiness for the procession. Suddenly it seemed as if the three dark figures were walking on a path of smoldering red fire, surrounded by darkness.

"They are so old and . . . small," said Mother, "I am glad Márton didn't let them go alone. And look, there is Jancsi!" she cried. "How big he is!"

"He must have been riding like the wind!" exclaimed Kate. "See him, Daddy? He does look handsome on that horse, even if he is my cousin!"

She laughed up at her father, her finger still pointing to Jancsi, who had just ridden into the pool of light. Then she sighed and shook him a little. "Daddy! What is it? You have got your schoolteacher face on."

"Have I? Well, then I might as well get it out of my system. Listen, little monkey. I want you to remember what Auntie just said; that she is glad Brother didn't let the Mandelbaums go alone. And remember what I am saying now—today, on the twenty-eighth of June 1914, to be exact—that I hope that tall farmer will always be there to help those two old people home."

He looked at Kate's intent little face and smiled. "Confound those red torches, they always make me act like a prophet with a long white beard! I was just talking to myself, Kate. Don't blink at me like a little old owl."

"I know Jancsi will always be there," said Kate, still looking at him.

"Jancsi? Where?"

Kate laughed. "Just talking to myself, Mr. Schoolmaster!

For you to remember." She whirled away before he could answer. "Here comes the first wagon with the gypsies! Come, Auntie. Come on, Daddy. I want to see everything. Look, they're bringing the furniture. Come on!"

The climax of all Hungarian country weddings, the "Lead Me Home," had begun. Men loaded all the bride's belongings into wagons. First came the freshly painted, gay new furniture. Then came homespun linens, sheets, pillowcases, curtains, tablecloths—dozens and dozens of everything, the product of twenty years of spinning, weaving, sewing. Dishes, cooking utensils, wooden implements came next, filling another wagon to the brim. The next one was loaded with food, bags and barrels of it. After all Mari's belongings had been packed into wagons, the guests piled into their own vehicles and the long procession began. The gypsies went ahead, playing favorite old songs and marches all the way. Each following wagon was lighted by six torches, except the last one, in which Mari and Peter were riding. The young couple were being led home; they didn't need a light—there was half a mile of blazing light and heart-warming music to follow.

Peter's farm was quite a distance from the village, and by the time he and Mari arrived the house was ready for them. Furniture had been placed, the bed made, the table set for two; the guests had even fed the chickens, pigs, and the cow. When Mari and Peter alighted, the first "caller" took them by the hand and led them over the threshold. They stood there, inside their home, waiting for the parting words of the caller; words without which no wedding was complete. Again the guests stood in a half-circle and the caller began to speak.

"Peter and Mari Hódi, may the Lord bless you and your home. May the Lord give you good health and happiness, long life, peace and prosperity, and may He send you children, grandchildren, and great-grandchildren, as many as there are stars in the sky."

He reached for the doorknob, and as he closed the door he said: "May this door keep all worry, all sadness and strife out of your house forever and after. Good night."

"I liked that part best of all, what he said about the door," spoke Kate sleepily out of a long silence when they were driving away. "I always like to close the door at night . . ."

Nobody answered; all were too tired to talk. By the time the wagon rolled into the village, even Kate was nodding with sleep. This was one time she didn't envy Jancsi, who was riding; Mother's lap was nice and soft to lean on. She wasn't very much interested in the unexpected stop they made in front of Uncle Moses' house, either. Through waves of drowsiness she heard a brief conversation and understood that Aaron had arrived. Moaning a little as she snuggled into a more comfortable position, she opened her eyes and saw a pale, keen-faced man, no doubt Aaron, lean against the wagon. He was talking to Uncle Márton and Kate heard the words: "pretty bad news." Then more droning talk and suddenly her father's voice, sharp and harsh: "Oh, God save us now!"

"What . . . what is it, Daddy?" She struggled up, frightened. Mother was asleep and the men didn't answer. "What happened?" she asked again. Jancsi leaned down from his horse. "It's nothing. I mean, not to us. He was just telling Father that Francis Ferdinand had been shot this afternoon—somewhere in Bosnia."

"Oh," sighed Kate, relieved that nothing more serious had happened. "Francis . . . what? Funny name for a horse."

"Horse nothing. He was the Crown Prince or something . . . Pali was telling us about him the other day. He said . . . oh, I can't remember, I'm tired. I wish they'd stop talking and go home." Jancsi sounded cross.

"Uhum," yawned Kate, settling down again. The wagon started and for a moment or two she was conscious of the dark houses along the street.

"All the nice little doors closed tight," she thought, "to keep out all worry and sadness and strife. . . ."

She smiled and fell asleep.

 CHAPTER V

FOR CONSPICUOUS BRAVERY . . .

LILY had been at the farm now for almost two months. The day after the wedding her father brought her out, a sulky, silent Lily, dressed in a plain blue dress that made her look what she was, a little girl. She suffered Mother's hearty kiss without responding with even so much as a smile, and Kate might as well have been thin air for all the attention Lily paid to her. When Mother led her into the house to show her the room she had fixed up "for my summer-baby," Father turned to Judge Kormos. "Don't look so worried, Béla; she'll get used to us and have a good time."

"Oh, it isn't that," sighed the Judge. "She didn't mind coming here; I know she enjoyed her short visit with you at Easter. It's those confounded puppies she had lost her heart to."

"What puppies?"

"Well," puffed Judge Kormos, easing his bulky frame onto a bench under the apple tree, "last night when I went to Váradi's—with my heart in my boots, to be frank—to take her home, I fully expected one of her tantrums. After all, she had never been dumped into a pile of straw before! And you know what I found? There she was, nestled into the straw with Váradi's old dog licking her face and a lapful of pups swarming all over that precious 'Paris model' of a dress. Then Váradi had to speak out of turn and tell her she could have the whole litter for all he cared, and . . . and then the tantrum came! We had to peel those puppies off her; they yelped and their mother howled and Lily outyowled the lot of them. . . ." He wiped his forehead. "I tell you, Márton, it was a riot!"

"Did she want them?"

"Want them! It's all she thinks and talks about, but . . ."

"Little fat ones?" breathed Kate, turning an eager face to Judge Kormos. He chuckled, smiling at the thought of those puppies himself. "Little fat leaky ones . . . all brown silk fuzz."

"Well, then, why didn't you bring one along for Lily?" asked Father. He sent a sidelong glance toward Kate. "Or two."

"Three," grinned Jancsi, pointing to himself. "I've never had a puppy. Peti was an old dog and now he is dead. Three, Father? Good! Can I go and get them . . . right now?"

"Me too . . . please, Uncle Márton!" pleaded Kate, tugging at his sleeve. He looked at Judge Kormos, laughing. "Will you trust Jancsi with your horse and buggy? He is a careful driver."

"I'd trust Jancsi with anything," nodded the Judge, "and I thank you, Márton, for . . ." But Kate and Jancsi didn't hear the rest. They were already in the buggy and off.

When a couple of hours later they drove into the yard, they saw Lily leaning against the well, kicking idly at clumps of grass.

"Hey, Lily!" called Kate. "Look what we got!"

Lily shrugged and turned her head away. Jancsi threw the reins around the hitching post and lifted a basket out of the buggy. A chorus of yipping complaint started up inside and Lily spun around. "What . . . what have you got there?" she asked, her voice half eager, half suspicious. Jancsi set down the basket on the shady grass under the apple tree. He winked at Kate because Lily was coming, reluctantly at first, then with a sudden rush. "Puppies. . . . Why, they are my puppies!" she cried, falling on her knees beside the basket. She reached in with both hands and lifted one out, pressing it to her face.

"This one, he chewed my ear yesterday. Look, he knows me! See? He's chewing me again." She laughed, her face shining with happiness. Then, as Kate beamed back at her, she frowned. "Are they yours?"

"We can each have one," said Kate. "You pick yours first because you found them."

Lily gave a little squeal of joy. "This is mine, this little nibbling rascal. Oh, I'm so happy now! You know, I've never had a puppy and I always wanted one!"

"So did I," said Kate and Jancsi together, each reaching for a puppy. Lily opened her eyes wide. "Honest? I thought you had all kinds of pets here—chickens, lambs, horses."

"Sure, but you can't hold a horse in your lap and squeeze him like this. . . . Oooh!" Jancsi began to laugh. "Well, it's a good thing you can't do that to a horse . . . your pet is leaking."

"They do!" giggled Lily. "You should have seen my dress yesterday, but I don't mind." She turned over on her stomach and rubbed her face against the squirming puppy. "Rascal. I'll call him Rascal. What will you call yours?"

"Wags!" cried Jancsi, pointing at his puppy's tiny rear end. It was trying to wag its tail but his whole round self wagged with it.

"I'll call mine Friend," decided Kate and smiled to herself. She turned over too and Jancsi followed suit. The three heads bent over the puppies, close together.

"Rascal, Wags, and Friend," sighed Lily contentedly. Then, without looking up, she pushed Kate a little with her shoulder. "I was awful mad at you yesterday, but I'm not now. This is fun!"

The cousins' eyes met for a moment; it was a brief glance but its meaning was clear to both. Maybe Lily wasn't going to be so bad after all!

"Want to see my chickens?" To an outsider this would have been just a casual question, but all three knew that it was a peace treaty.

"We could teach you to ride if you'd like to." Jancsi was doing his share too. "Then we could all go and see my herd."

"And the lambs . . . hundreds and thousands of them, Lily, like a big white cloud rolling over the meadows. And Pista would tell us stories, nice, creepy ones. And . . ."

The three heads pressed closer together and three pairs of legs were kicking and waving in the air. In the center of it all the three puppies went peacefully to sleep, not at all disturbed by the giggle-interspersed talk over their heads.

By the time Mother called them in for the noonday meal, the three children had made plans enough not for one summer but for ten. They prattled on all through the meal, unmindful of the amused glances of the grown-ups. Only Jancsi noticed that toward the end of the meal the men's conversation had taken a serious turn; that the jovial round face of Judge Kormos had lost its smile, and Father was frowning. Strange words, sinister words his ear had absorbed while his thoughts were still on their childish plans, echoed in his mind now; words with a vaguely ugly meaning. "Assassination . . . rights of minorities . . . ultimatum to Serbia . . . mobilization. War. WAR?

Uncle Sándor rose and began to pace the room, up and down, up and down. "I tell you," he cried, "the government is playing with fire! If Austria declares war and we are dragged into it, this country is doomed."

The Judge grunted. "Bah! We would crush the Serbs"—he pressed a broad thumbnail down on a crumb of bread—"like this. In two weeks it would be all over."

"And why should we?" demanded Uncle Sándor hotly. "What have we got against the Serbs? Just because a fanatic, a misled, misguided youngster has killed the man who was the symbol of Austrian threats, Austrian greed and domination, is that reason enough for plunging two countries into war? Would a war give his life back to him?" His voice broke, his hands dropped, and he began to pace the room again.

Jancsi's puzzled eyes turned to Father. He was still frowning, his face set and dark, more serious than Jancsi had ever seen it. He was looking straight at Jancsi but it was many moments before a glimmer of a smile showed in his eyes and then it came slowly as if it had to fight its way through dark clouds of worry.

"Jancsi, why don't you and Kate show Lily the garden? She could pick some flowers for Judge Kormos to take home," he said. "Run along!" he added almost impatiently when Jancsi didn't move. Then gently: "Run along, Son, while the sun is still shining."

The children went. As the door closed on them, Kate laughed. "Uncle Márton must be all mixed up; it's only noon, and the sun won't go down for . . . ages! Tell you what! Let's go down to the brook first and pick forget-me-nots." She looked at Jancsi. "Hey, old somberface, what are *you* frowning about?"

"What your father said . . ." began Jancsi, but she tweaked his nose. "Oh, Daddy? He is forever preaching; don't you know him yet? Come on."

That was two months ago. Since then the puppies had

grown to almost twice their size; now they were awkward little dogs, rollicking, romping, getting into everybody's way and chewing to rags everything chewable. Three little clowns who could bring laughter to Father's face and sometimes chase away the worried wrinkles from Sándor Nagy's forehead. Not always. For, in those two months those vaguely sinister words, ultimatum, mobilization, war, had become realities for all. Hungary was at war. Not only Hungary; all Europe. Since July 28, when Austria-Hungary had declared war on Serbia, every day, every mail that reached the village, had brought news of more and more countries declaring war on one another: Russia against Austria-Hungary, Germany against France, England against Germany. At first this news was only words too, little black words printed on paper, but as time went on they took on life and began to move, became the marching feet of men, the rumbling wheels of trains and cannon.

One evening after supper, at the end of a blazing, breathless August day, the family was sitting under the apple tree. They had been out in the wheatfields since dawn. Even Lily had worked along with Kate, carrying water to the hired men and women, helping to take care of babies whom their mothers had brought along. It had been the last day of harvest; now all the wheat- and ryefields lay bare and brown and the barns were full of golden grain.

Lily rolled over and over on the grass, trying to hide her sunburned nose from Rascal's too friendly tongue. She sat up, hugging the ecstatic little dog to her. "Oh, Rascal, isn't this fun? Honestly"—she sent a shining smile at Father—"I've never been this happy in my life, Uncle Márton. I don't want to go back to that school. Couldn't I stay . . . please . . . forever and ever and ever?"

Father smiled and rumpled her already rumpled blond curls. "That isn't for me to say, Lily. We would like to keep you . . . forever and ever and ever . . . but you'll have to ask your father."

Lily pouted. "You can't talk to him now. He always looks as black as thunder and talks about drafts and enlistments and things. War is a nuisance, anyway! It changes people."

"To say the least," said Kate's father with a dry little chuckle. Father only sighed. He had been answering questions all day, the worried, puzzled questions of his men. "What are they fighting about, Mr. Nagy?" "Do we have to go to war too?" "Will I have to leave my wife, children? What will become of them? Who will take care of them?"

They all came to him and he answered as well as he could, promising to take care of their families in case they'd have to go, but evading the one question that was uppermost in their minds: "What are they fighting about?" To that he didn't know the answer.

His thoughts were interrupted by one sharp bark and two answering growls. Rascal, Wags, and Friend broke away from the family circle and galumped across the yard, making enough noise for one medium-sized watchdog. Jancsi peered through the hazy dusk. "It's your father's buggy, Lily. Hello! Over here, Judge Kormos, under the tree!" he shouted.

A dark figure alighted from the buggy and moved toward the tree. Father rose and said:

"That isn't Judge Kormos . . . he's too thin. Aaron, is that you?"

Spurs clinked and Aaron said in a low voice: "Reserve Lieutenant Aaron Mandelbaum since this morning. I have been called. . . ."

"Another wedding?" cried Kate and clapped her hands against her lips as the truth suddenly dawned on her. The dark eyes in Aaron's face turned toward her. He smiled. "I wish it were, little Kate. Or maybe it is," he added in a strange voice, "the Devil's own wedding, with Death for a fiddler." Then he addressed himself to Father again: "I received orders to take the first unit out of our territory tomorrow. All men between twenty-two and thirty. I am to take them to Budapest for distribution to their own regiments. Then I have to join my regiment on the Russian front. We leave . . . at noon," he added after a little silence.

Márton Nagy brushed his hand across his forehead. "Let's go inside. I want to talk to you."

"I'd rather not," said Aaron almost gruffly. "I have to go right back . . . I only came to ask you to come in tomorrow . . . if you can."

"Why, of course we'll come to see you off. We will all go in!" cried Mother.

"Thank you. I hoped you would. I . . . counted on it." Aaron's voice sounded strangely constrained and they couldn't see his face now. "I may not have time to say good-by tomorrow or ask you to do a great favor for me . . . so I am asking you now."

"Anything we can do . . ." began Father.

"I know. This"—he held out a white envelope to Father—"this is the favor. Please open it after I have left. Not before. I want you to promise. *Not* before I am out of the village!"

"Of course . . . I promise," said Father, taking the envelope. Aaron sighed deeply. "You will understand why I am burdening you with this. It takes a strong man to carry that envelope where it has to go, stronger than I am. And so I will just say 'Until we meet again,' and thank you."

He went, spurs clinking across the dark yard, and soon the yellow lanterns on the buggy disappeared between the poplars on the lane.

And so next morning the family left again to drive into the village with a wagonful of flowers. Kate and Lily had gathered all the blazing red and yellow zinnias, roses, deep blue cornflowers, fragrant rosemary, sweet mignonette; they stripped the garden of all its bloom to make up countless small, tight bouquets. There were enough for all the men who were leaving, enough to throw under the horses' feet as the wagons, filled with singing, waving men, began to roll out of the village. All the little gardens must have been stripped bare, because when the wagons had disappeared behind clouds of dust, the whole long village street was covered with flowers.

Uncle Moses was still waving, long after Aaron had ridden off behind the last wagon. He wiped his eyes stealthily. "Don't cry, Mama." He smiled into Aunt Sarah's brimming eyes.

"Don't you cry. Be glad, like I am! Our son makes a fine Hungarian officer; he is going to fight for our country, Mama. Be proud of him!"

Kate turned around—they had all been standing in front of the store—and saw that Aunt Sarah was groping for a hand-kerchief. She made a move to give her one, but Lily was quicker. Lily, her own eyes brimming, had one arm around Aunt Sarah's shoulders and was wiping her face gently.

"He wore your flowers over his heart," Lily was saying, "did you see, Aunt Sarah? And he let me kiss him good-by too. I kissed all of them good-by . . . for luck."

The glances of Kate and Jancsi met, and parted to exchange brief messages of surprise with the rest of the family. They all thought the same thing, but only Jancsi put it into words. "Who would have believed that?" he said, shaking his head a little as if he still couldn't believe what he saw. Somewhere, somehow in the past two months they had lost "that Lily," the flouncing, peevish, bored Lily, and found this sunburned little girl to whom Aunt Sarah was clinging now, saying: "I am sure it will bring them luck, my child."

People began to drift back to their homes and Mother was getting restless. "I've got to do my washing today or you won't have a clean shirt for Sunday," she reminded Father. They were driving out of the village when Father stopped the horses and drew Aaron's white envelope out of his pocket. "Let's see what this mysterious package is," he smiled, ripping it open. A small golden disk with a red ribbon on it fell out and clattered on the wagon floor. Jancsi picked it up. " 'For

. . . conspicuous . . . bravery . . . in the . . . presence of the enemy,' " he read slowly, turning the little shining disk around and around. Then he looked up quickly because Mother was asking: "What is it, Márton? What is it?" and Father began to read from the slip of white paper he held in his hand:

" 'It is the sad duty of the War Department to inform you that your brother, Rabbi Joseph Mandelbaum, was killed in the first battle on the Russian front, while administering aid to the wounded caught between the firing lines.' "

The last words were hardly more than a whisper, drowned in the silence around him. Only the paper rustled as he folded it up carefully, slowly, because his fingers were trembling. The midday sun beat down on the endless plains; heat rose from the shorn fields and shimmered over the brown stubble. Farther away sheep were grazing and from the scant shade of a lone tree came the plaintive, silvery sound of a shepherd's flute. A lark, envious perhaps of the sweet sounds, burst into song, flinging its small body into the air, soaring higher and higher until its song seemed to drift down from heaven itself.

"Little thin Joseph with the silver voice," said Kate's father. "Remember, Márton, when we went to school together and the old teacher used to begin every morning with singing? The 'Magyar Hymn.' We all used to stand up and bellow our lungs out at first, but Joseph always finished it alone. We just had to listen to that soaring voice of his that could turn a song into a prayer. . . . Remember?"

Father remembered. He rose and began to say the words of the "Magyar Hymn":

"God bless all Hungarians
With freedom, joy, prosperity . . ."

Somehow the tune crept into his voice and then all of them
were singing, standing with bared heads and folded hands.

"Help us with Thy protecting arms
When we fight our enemy . . ."

The lone shepherd must have heard them, because long
after the hymn was ended, his silvery flute echoed the tune
and the invisible lark trilled an accompaniment to it from
the sky.

"Son," said Father huskily, "you drive home. I have to go
back to do what Aaron couldn't do."

"I am coming with you," said Mother. The others looked
after them as they walked back slowly, arm in arm, treading
the path of now withered and dusty flowers. Márton Nagy's
shoulders were bowed as if he were carrying a heavy weight.
Into Kate's mind flashed a memory of just two short months
ago and she glanced at her father's face. He must have been
thinking the same thing because he said:

"That tall farmer will never let the Mandelbaums go alone."

 CHAPTER VI

CORPORAL NAGY

SUMMER was gone. Autumn slipped away and with it went the hope so many men had voiced: "We will be home for Christmas." Winter came, then spring, and with the melting snow more and more men went away to the ever-growing war.

Old Arpád was almost the only herder left and he didn't have very much to do because the great corrals were nearly empty. Father had had to sell most of his horses to the Army; he kept only a few mares, one stallion, and horses too young to be broken in. And Jancsi's herd.

The six tiny foals were yearlings now; they roamed the pastures independent of their mothers, six proud-stepping, glossy-coated young horses, Jancsi's great pride and joy. He couldn't spend half as much time with them as he would have liked to; there were too many other things to do. He didn't even have time to notice how many of the responsibilities of running a big ranch had come to rest on his shoulders. Father was always there, of course; the two of them were almost inseparable. But Father no longer gave orders to Jancsi; he only suggested what should be done. That was all right. What Jancsi resented was that Father, his father, had taken to keeping books. Evenings, after the family had gone to bed, Father would bring out a fat ledger to pore over it, his pen scratching away in the silence of the kitchen for hours.

One night Jancsi woke up. He felt that it must be very late and yet there was a light seeping into his room. He slipped out of bed and padded noiselessly into the kitchen. A candle, burned almost to its last drops of tallow, was spluttering on the table. Father had fallen asleep, his arms stretched across the open pages. Jancsi rubbed his sleep-swimming eyes and glanced at the cuckoo-clock on the shelf. Two o'clock! Almost morning.

"Father!" He shook his father's shoulder crossly. "You are worse than . . ." Words failed Jancsi as Father's blurred, heavy eyes looked up at him. Then because that beloved face was so pitifully tired, he made his voice sound very gruff: "We planned to start haying tomorrow and now it's already today and . . . honestly, Father"—he sank into a chair and jabbed an accusing thumb at the book—"what did you start that for? We didn't need books before!"

"Well, maybe I am getting old, Son. Old people like to play with new things," smiled Father, stretching his arms wide and yawning hugely. Then he flipped the book shut and leaned his elbows on it. "Some time when you just feel like 'improving your mind,' as Brother would say, you might look into this. It doesn't bite!" he chuckled as Jancsi made a face.

"Huh. You keep it locked away."

"Yes, I have. But"—something clattered onto the table— "but, young master, here is the key. You can lock it up yourself now and . . . keep the key. I won't need it for quite a while."

"That's good," sighed Jancsi. He locked the book in the cupboard where Father kept his gun and stood twirling the key around his finger. "Throw it in the well?" he grinned.

"I wouldn't," Father smiled back, rising from his chair. "Now run back to bed; I am going to catch a little cat nap myself."

The morning was bright and clear with the shining, spotless freshness of early June mornings. Jancsi was eager to be off and start the haying and he fidgeted impatiently all through breakfast. Such a made-to-order day for work on the fields and there was Father talking about unimportant things like vegetables and fruit, things that could just as well be discussed after the day's work was done. Jancsi frowned at Lily; she had started it with some silly complaint about Máli the old cow's not giving enough milk. Then he shook his head, disapproving of his own cross thought about Lily. She was all right; he was glad she hadn't gone back to school. For all he heard, Budapest was no place for a girl these days, with everybody crazy about this war business, with the soldiers on leave drinking and carousing (at least that was what Judge Kormos had said before he went away to the war), and with her mother still so sick in the hospital. . . .

"What did you say, Father? I wasn't listening."

"So I noticed," smiled Father. "I was saying that we need a new cow. See Uncle Moses the next time you go to the village; he'll find us a good one."

"Cows!" exploded Jancsi, with such contempt in his voice that Father began to laugh.

"Well, since Lily has taken that hateful job of milking off your hands, the least you can do is give her a good one to milk. Take Kate with you. Kate," he spoke to her, "Uncle Moses said something about a new preservative for eggs. You had better talk to him too and let him order some. Egg prices will go still higher."

"Oh, Márton, it can't last forever," sighed Mother, her voice small and tight.

"Not forever," said Father. "They seem to have settled down to it, though; it might last quite a while."

"Márton! With all the men away, what will we do? I live in fear . . . any day one of those dreadful yellow cards might come . . . calling you in . . . taking *you* away. Márton, if I see that card, I'll just die."

"Now, now, old lady, that is no way to talk." His voice sounded forcedly cheerful, almost too loud. When she didn't smile, he prodded her under the chin, lifting her bowed head. "I assure you, Mother, that none of those yellow cards will come into your house. Now smile!"

"You mean . . . they won't take you?" whispered Mother, smiling through her tears.

"Bah. Nobody can take me anywhere. I go where I want to go or . . . have to go, but take me? No!"

"*I* will, if you sit here gossiping much longer," grumbled Jancsi. Father chuckled. "Horses saddled?"

"Hours ago!"

"Well, then . . ." Father rose reluctantly, almost pulling himself erect. As he straightened up, his eyes roamed around the old kitchen, making brief little stops on the gaily painted cupboards, the fat white stove, the flowerbench under the window. It was so unusual for him to linger that Mother looked at him with narrowing eyes.

"Márton, you are as pale as a ghost. Are you ill?"

"Sitting up all night, playing with books . . . ask your son!" he smiled. He laid an arm around Mother's waist, held out his other hand to the girls. "Come, little monkeys, help a poor old man to the door."

"Ooooh, Uncle Márton, but you are strong!" gasped Kate when he let them go at the door.

"You gave us a real bear hug; you . . . you hurt!"

"Ah, poor pussy, come, I'll kiss you to make it well." He bent and kissed the tip of her nose, then quickly kissed Lily. "You too. And you old lady," he chuckled, giving Mother a resounding kiss.

"Well, I never . . . you big baby, you! Go on, go on now, or Jancsi will lay you across his knee." She laughed, pushing him toward the stable. After the riders had gone she smiled down at Kate. "I've never seen him so full of fun; play-acting like a big baby."

"It's nice," said Lily. "Most everybody else is so cross and grumpy now . . . I wish somebody would stop this war."

"Oh, dear!" sighed Mother, her eyes troubled again. "It doesn't seem possible, does it? All this beautiful sunshine, birds singing, little plants growing all around us, and out there . . . somewhere, men are killing each other. I am thankful that at least we can't hear the guns."

"Daddy," said Kate in a choked voice, and Mother drew both girls close. "He is safe, lamb. He is far away in Russia . . . but he is safe."

"Prisoners must be better off than we are," said Lily solemnly. "I hope, I hope that Father will be taken too. They don't have to wait . . . and worry. And when the war is over, they'll just . . . just go home."

"Mmmm," crooned Mother, "everybody will go home; there will be singing and dancing again and our men working in the fields. Women will go back to their kitchens to cook for them instead of plowing and reaping. Why, it isn't even seemly to see a woman behind a heavy plow! The whole world is turned upside down. It must be," she cried, "with all of us mooning here instead of doing our chores! What would Jancsi say!"

"That bossy thing!" smiled Kate. "He thinks he owns the world the way he orders everybody around, even Uncle Márton."

"He is doing a man's work too," sighed Mother. "I know he will be as hungry as a wolf again—haying all day is hard work for a boy."

But Jancsi wasn't haying. He didn't know he wasn't going to until after they had turned into the lane. There Father reined in his horse and rode slowly, looking back at the house.

"Son," he said as Jancsi, his face a picture of disapproval, galloped back to him, "we won't start haying today. We'll ride into town; I have some things to do that cannot wait."

"Town?" Jancsi's frown melted away. "Hurrah!" This was going to be a holiday; a trip to town always was, it happened so seldom. He didn't question this sudden change of plans, only commented: "If I had known that, I would have worn my blue suit. Maybe we'll eat in one of those restaurants?"

Father said they would, most certainly. They would just have one big time together, a man's party. "We'll eat all the ice cream we want for once"—he winked at Jancsi—"without Mother worrying about stomach-aches."

"Raspberry and vanilla and apricot and chocolate and orange?"

"And lemon and coffee and strawberry, with lots of nuts and whipped cream."

"And castor oil when we get home," finished Jancsi making a wry face but with his eyes shining.

"Who cares?" laughed Father.

They didn't stop in the village. Father seemed to be in a hurry now; he didn't look either to left or to right but rode straight through, his spurs digging into Bátor's sides. Then they were in the open country again, the dusty white road between village and town stretching ahead of them like a white ribbon laid on the green velvet of the fields.

Soon the tall buildings and chimneys of the town loomed up, then the horses' hoofs were clattering on the cobbled streets. They left the horses in a livery stable near the railroad station and walked into the center of the town. Jancsi had been to town only three times in his life; the tall houses, large plate-glass windows, and the bustle of many hurrying strangers were still a novelty to him. Craning his neck, gaping into store-windows, he bumped into people left and right. Father took his arm. "This is where we are going," he said, opening the door of a large building. "Town Hall" was printed on the door, and many small rooms opened off the long corridor inside.

"The clerk is waiting for you, Mr. Nagy," said a boy to whom Father had given his name. Then they were standing in one of the small rooms. It smelled of dust and ink so badly that Jancsi sneezed.

"So this is the young fellow," said the old man behind the desk, peering at Jancsi over his spectacles. "Pretty young for what's in here, Mr. Nagy." He tapped a folded paper in front of him.

"Young but level-headed. He will be all right," said Father, laying a hand on Jancsi's shoulder.

"Humph. Too bad ... this war ..." The clerk shook his head

sadly, then pushed the paper across the desk. "Just sign this, both of you."

Father signed his name rapidly. "Write your name here, young fellow," said the clerk, pointing to a dotted line. Jancsi hesitated, then shook his head resolutely. "I'll read what it says first."

The old clerk's mouth fell open. "Well, I never! Who taught you that?"

"Nobody. I . . . I heard when Uncle Moses scolded Aunt Vidor. She was crying and he said she deserved to be cheated. He said only a fool would sign a paper without reading it first. I am not a fool," he added solemnly.

The clerk slapped his thigh. "He'll do, Mr. Nagy!" he exclaimed. Father was looking at Jancsi. "I'll explain, Son. This paper gives you the right to buy or sell anything on the farm: animals, grain, food—whatever we need—without asking me first. You know how busy we are now—sometimes I may not be home when the buyers come, and this will save time."

A whistle escaped Jancsi. "You mean . . . I can do anything you would do?"

"Practically," smiled Father.

"Whew! Gimme that pen!" He signed his name in round, sprawling letters. "Wait till I tell Kate . . . and Mother and Lily! Whew!"

He jumped up, hooked his thumbs into his vest-pockets, and began to strut, grinning broadly.

"Well, that's that," said Father, slipping the paper into prancing Jancsi's pocket. "Hang onto this."

"Don't worry; I'll sleep with it under my pillow."

"Good luck to you, Mr. Nagy, and to you, young fellow," said the clerk when they were leaving. "Give my regards to Uncle Moses."

"You know him?" beamed Jancsi.

"No, but I'd like to. He sounds like a good friend for a young man like you to have."

"He is," said Father over Jancsi's vigorously assenting head. "I always take his advice, and so will Jancsi."

Then they were out in the sunshine again, among the jostling crowd. There were soldiers in uniform everywhere, strolling or hurrying along the sidewalks, behind the windows of cafés and restaurants. Long columns of soldiers were marching on every street, and once in a while heavy artillery trucks rumbled and clattered toward the railroad station.

"Cannon," said Father when Jancsi gaped at the unearthly-looking, canvas-wrapped monsters on the trucks. "They could throw a shell from here to the farm and shatter the house."

"Not our house. They wouldn't!" exclaimed Jancsi, casting a threatening glance at the cannon.

"No, not our house, thank the Lord," sighed Father. "But they will shatter houses like ours somewhere, wherever they are going. Little peaceful white houses in Serbia or Russia . . . homes of little peaceful people such as we are." He had been speaking in a low voice, then unexpectedly he asked: "Remember the round-up, Jancsi? When you and Kate got caught in the stampede?"

"Do I!"

"War is like a stampede, Jancsi. A small thing can start it and suddenly the very earth is shaking with fury and people turn into wild things, crushing everything beautiful and sweet, destroying homes, lives, blindly in their mad rush from nowhere to nowhere. A stampede, a mad whirlwind that sucks in men like those marching so bravely"—his eyes followed the endless column of soldiers—"and spits them out when they are . . . like that." Two crippled men in uniform passed them on crutches, sad, tired eyes staring vacantly ahead.

"I . . . hate it!" said Jancsi between clenched teeth, with all the flaming, scornful conviction of a boy who has grown up to respect life and healthy strength in plants, animals, and people. To make things *live*, and to keep them alive, had always been his life and now he was face to face with a dark power that destroyed life and health. He couldn't understand it, he could only hate it.

"Everybody hates it, but we are caught in the stampede and we'll have to see it through." Father's smile broke through the gloom his words had cast. "How about a great big meal now, Son? Make us feel better."

Jancsi ate sparingly of all the strange dishes, saving plenty of room for the promised ice cream. Even so there was a limit to the capacity of his stomach; he had to give up after the orange ice. But, since Father had ordered different flavors for himself, he had a taste of every kind. They leaned back, laughing at each other.

"I'm so heavy in the middle, I can't get up from this chair," groaned Jancsi.

"Well, then, stay where you are. I have to do some things, anyway; wait for me here, Son."

Father asked the waiter to bring Jancsi picture magazines to look at, and left.

Jancsi was engrossed with the magazines. He had never seen any before. The pictures of the theaters, of Budapest, of foreign countries were like a fairyland opening up for him. War pictures he paged over frowningly. He hated war. But the photograph of a familiar face arrested his eyes and he yelled out: "Judge Kormos!"

Faces turned toward him from every table. He was on his feet, waving the magazine.

"Judge Kormos . . . look, look, everybody! He got . . . he"— Jancsi scanned the printed lines again—"he got the Iron Cross from the German Kaiser himself"—another glance—"for conspicuous bravery before the enemy. But he isn't dead!" He cried as the words brought back, in a flash of memory, that sad day when Aaron went away. "No, sir! He was promoted too. Look, he is a major!"

He pushed the magazine into the face of anybody who wanted to look and his enthusiasm made everybody want to.

"That's great, Son," said an officer, smiling. "Who is he?"

"Friend of mine," declared Jancsi. "He is the Judge. Lily's father, you know."

"I see. And who are you, young fellow?"

"Why . . . why . . ." Jancsi blinked, surprised at the thought that anybody should be so ignorant as not to know who he was. "Jancsi Nagy, of course."

More questions followed, revealing the fact that all these people were sadly in need of information. Why, they didn't know *anything!* Then, not waiting for any more questions, he was prattling for all he was worth, words gushing out of him. The farm, Father, Kate, Lily, his herd, the dogs, Uncle Moses—all he loved came to life to these strange listeners whose number grew as he talked on. He didn't know that in this railroad town whence thousands of singing men went away every day and into which hundreds of silent, maimed ones were sent back, his words had created a little island of almost forgotten peace. Men and women, young and old were living, for a few brief moments, on a sun-drenched farm, far, far away from the dreadful roaring of guns. Jancsi didn't know this; he was simply talking about things he loved. The big clock on the wall ticked away the minutes, but no one noticed until a deep voice broke the spell.

"What's going on here? Jancsi! What are you doing?" It was Father's voice and Jancsi turned, the Judge's picture waving again, to flutter unnoticed and forgotten to the floor.

"Father!" Jancsi said in a choking voice, looking at him with eyes that stared from a face slowly draining of color. For Father didn't look like his father now; the drab gray of the uniform he wore made him look like one small part of that endless column of marching men.

"Corporal?" said the officer gently, and Father saluted.

"Corporal Márton Nagy of the Seventh Infantry, sir," he said. The officer glanced at the clock. "You have but half an hour. . . ."

Father looked down at Jancsi and smiled a fleeting smile before he answered: "I know, sir. We will be there on time."

He raised his hand to his cap again, then took Jancsi by the shoulder. "Come, Son."

Somehow Jancsi's feet began to move and he was walking beside his Father through a blurred mass of houses, streets, people. Then they were sitting on a bench, in a quiet corner of the railroad station. Father held his arm in a tight grip and said:

"Chin up, young fellow. This is the castor oil."

"You *knew* . . . all day you knew!" Jancsi faltered, strange bits of the day's happenings suddenly falling into place.

"I've known it for quite a while, Son. What I didn't want was anyone crying over me. That's why I didn't tell."

Jancsi clenched his teeth. "I am not crying."

"Men don't. And now, Jancsi," Father said as the whistle of a distant train floated in, "I am going to ask you to do something . . . man to man. Stand up straight and look at me."

"Yes, sir."

"That's a good soldier. See that door, Son? When I say 'Forward, march,' you march right through that door, across the street to the stable, get the horses, and ride on home. Without once looking back."

"Y-yes, sir."

The train whistle sounded again, this time much louder.

"Soldier, forward, march!" Father's voice seemed to come from a great distance, drowned in the clatter of many heavy boots, of the loudening clamor of the approaching train. Jancsi

marched blindly through the noise and the crowd, through the door, and across the street. Left-right, left-right, his own boots clumped on the wooden floor of the stable. Then he was on Bársony, leading Father's horse. Behind him he heard the snorting gasps of an engine, shrill whistles, and the hoarse shouts of many men, and he dug his spurs deeply into Bársony's sides. He never looked back. He never slackened the pace of the racing horses until they were pounding down the village street.

"Ride on home," Father had said, but suddenly Jancsi knew that he couldn't. Not yet. There was a burning ache inside him that made him shake all over. He couldn't take that home. He slipped off his horse and stumbled into the store, into the arms of the only friend who could help him now.

"Uncle Moses," he gasped after a flood of tears had eased that choking ache, "I couldn't cry at home. . . ."

"I know, Jancsi . . . I know," crooned Uncle Moses, rocking him back and forth. "You are the only man there now, you'll have to be strong. But, any time this business of being a man gets too much for you, just come to Uncle Moses."

Jancsi lifted a tear-stained but resolute face. "I can go home now." Then he frowned, trying to remember. "There was something . . . oh! Father said we need a new cow."

"Mmmm. A cow." Uncle Moses studied the ceiling. "Mmmm. And I need wool . . . and hides. Aha! I'll find a cow and next time you come in, we'll do business."

"Silver buttons?" Janci reminded him. Uncle Moses chuckled. "Something like that. Now go on home, Jancsi, but remember! Just come to Uncle Moses."

 CHAPTER VII

SIX BIG RUSSIANS

HAYING was a grueling job, even with strong men for help. With only women, old men, and boys of his own age to work with, Jancsi had all he could do to get the hay into the barns.

Then, before he knew it, harvesting was on his hands and later corn-cutting and potato-digging. Days took on wings and flew away, and he had no time to watch their flight. Nobody had and nobody wanted to. Time was something to be pushed ahead—hurry, hurry, hurry; people seemed to say to each new day: "Hurry," for then tomorrow would come and tomorrow might bring the end of the war. But as the seasons rolled by and the sun rose on a brand-new day every dawn, it was never the tomorrow they were all praying for.

Each day brought news; a see-saw of news, good and bad. Everybody had learned the sinister lingo of war: offensive, campaign, trench, submarine, airplane, bombs, gas. Dots on the map of Europe, with strange names such as Przemysl, Ypres, Brest-Litovsk, Paris—and later Isonzo, for Italy had been sucked into the war too—had become real places where guns threatened husbands and sons. Merely names before; now the very sound of them was a threat to everyone.

Mail came every day to the remote village now and the very color of the cards and envelopes handed out by Uncle Moses meant joy or grief for someone. A pink card placed into a trembling hand: "He is all right, thank God! He wrote it himself." A travel-worn, often-sealed envelope with the double-headed Russian eagle on it: "He is a prisoner, thank the Lord." The large white envelope, heavy with someone's small possessions who would never come back, and a woman would bow her head and go away weeping. There was no glory in this war; news of victories was not proclaimed with brass bands and flags flying; only mute, anxious eyes of helpless women and children asking: "What price, O Lord, what price victory?"

There were two growing stacks of pink cards in Mother's bureau drawer between the prayerbooks and the Bible, and a few travel-worn, many-sealed envelopes from Russia. She would bring them out to the kitchen every night and the four of them would read every one over and over again. They were all much the same, saying very little about the war, but reading them aloud would bring the three men closer. . . .

It was toward the end of the second year, in November 1915, that two cards from Father came on the same day.

" 'Don't be alarmed if you don't hear from me for a while. A bad storm is blowing up and it might wash out the roads,' " read Jancsi for the second time. He glanced up at Mother, ready to voice what seemed to him an explanation of this strange statement, that this storm was going to be one of those offensive drives. But Mother was smiling.

"He'll catch cold, that baby. I bet he never remembers to change his clothes if he gets soaked."

So Jancsi didn't say anything, just picked up the second card. "This is a funny one. It says: 'Dear Jancsi, Remember to put up enough sausages for Kate. Have you still got the key?' Sausages!" he grumbled. "Where will I get anyone to butcher . . . ?"

"What key?" Mother interrupted. "You are just like your Father, Jancsi; you never tell me anything."

Jancsi was already in his room and came back, brandishing a key. "This. He made me lock up the book and I have forgotten all about it."

They bent over the open book. As they began to read the closely written pages, their heads pressed together and there was no other sound for a long time but the rustle of turning leaves and the ticking of the cuckoo-clock. And once in a while the gentle splash of a tear falling on paper. But when Jancsi turned the last written page and looked up, his eyes weren't wet. They were shining with a light much brighter than the light of the candle.

"Why, Mother, he never left us at all! He has been here all this time and we didn't know it. Look, Mother, oh, Mother, he wrote us something for every day for almost a year ahead ... for all of us! And, Mother, I did all he wanted me to do ... the harvest, the corn, the sheep. We all did!"

"He thought of everything," whispered Mother, her finger on a page beginning with November 1915. 'Get old János Vidor to butcher the pigs.' Oh, Márton"—she straightened, gazing through the window into the night—"your son asked a question and you answered from across the miles. If you can hear us, Márton, listen, be careful of that storm ... oh, be so careful!"

So she knew, thought Jancsi. Under that gentle smile she was hiding the same fear, smiling so we wouldn't be frightened. Just as she was smiling when I came home without him and she said: I know, Jancsi. He kissed us good-by. ... So women were not all gentle, helpless softness, either; they too had a steel armor that would not let them show the tears inside.

The last shred of harsh, small-boyish pride in his new manhood left Jancsi then; he was all man now, bowing his head to the strength of a woman.

He bent over the book again. "He says here: 'October. Plow up some of the pastures for spring planting of more corn and potatoes. Ask Uncle Moses to make out an application for Russian prisoners if necessary.' " Jancsi looked up. "We could still do that plowing. Would you mind feeding prisoners, Mother?"

"Why should I mind? They are men, like ours. Maybe ...

if we are good to them . . . they'll write home too, like Sándor, and say that we are kind and maybe some Russian woman will say to her husband or son: 'Don't aim your gun too well; they are just simple people like we are.' "

"All right, Mother. How many can you feed?"

"As many as you need, Jancsi. It will be nice to cook again big caldrons full of stew, and bake large round loaves of bread. It . . . it'll fill up the time and keep me from thinking too much."

Barely two weeks later Uncle Moses told Jancsi that six prisoners would arrive next day. "Here is your approved application," he said. "The guard will bring them here. Come with the wagon tomorrow afternoon to take them home."

An uneasy thought assailed Jancsi. "How in the world will I talk to them?"

"They'll learn fast," smiled Uncle Moses. "A plow looks like a plow the world over; so does a horse. And I speak Russian, Jancsi. If you get in a tight spot, just come to Uncle Moses."

Jancsi smiled wryly. "That's all I do, it seems. So does everybody else in the village. No money, go to Uncle Moses. Can't read or write, Uncle Moses will do it. Sick? Uncle Moses will find a remedy. Want to bawl like a calf"—he pointed to himself—"Uncle Moses has a good shoulder to bawl on. We seem to . . . we seem to pack up all our troubles and dump them on your doorstep."

"Well, Jancsi, it's give and take that makes the world go around. I am paying a debt . . . we Jews are." He glanced at

Jancsi and, seeing the question on his face, went on: "Your great-grandfather and others in his time reached down into the dark despair we Jews had fallen into and lifted us up; made Hungarians out of us, given us a place in the sun. They didn't need us . . . then. Now, *you* do. And now, we pay, gladly. Joseph"—his voice hesitated for a moment then grew stronger than before—"Joseph my first-born son gave all he had, but I am proud, Jancsi . . . proud that he was allowed to."

A little silence fell on both of them. Then Uncle Moses said briskly: "Tomorrow afternoon, Jancsi, and bring in a few baskets of eggs. I can sell them at a good profit."

Next day before Jancsi left, he and Kate had a row. Kate was not going to let Jancsi take *her* eggs. She was going along. Jancsi argued and pleaded. He yelled at her. He tried to pull her off the wagon but she had entrenched herself between the baskets and all he got for trying was a kick in his arm.

Mother and Lily came running out of the house. Jancsi, nursing his arm, turned to Mother. "You tell her . . . you tell her that she can't ride home with six prisoners in the wagon! It'll be dark before we get home!"

Mother looked at Kate, but she only settled herself more firmly between the baskets and shook her head. "He can't boss me around. I am going."

"But, lamb, he is right. It isn't proper for a girl! You can go some other time."

It was no good. "I am going," was all Kate said. Then both Mother and Jancsi began to scold and even Lily put in a word or two, forthright words at that.

"You are just plain cussed, that's what you are. What do you want to go so almighty bad for just *exactly* today? What's that?" she asked curiously as Kate, stubbornly pulling her jacket tighter around her, revealed a large, flat package thus far hidden under her apron.

"None of your business, nosy!" flashed Kate, but suddenly changed her mind. "All right. If he hadn't hollered at me, I would have told anyway." She held up the package. It was a large photograph of her father she had had in her room.

"I thought . . . I wanted to see the prisoners right away. I . . . maybe one of them had . . . seen Daddy in Russia. So there. And I am going!"

"Of course you are, lamb," said Mother. "Lily, go get your jacket too. You are going with Kate."

Jancsi groaned. "Let's call the dogs and the chickens and take the cow, to make it complete."

Mother gave him one look and he hung his head. "Oh . . . all right. I'm sorry." He thawed out on the drive, though, and admitted that this was better than going alone.

The prisoners were already there when they arrived. Jancsi, with a horseman's expert eye, saw that they had good strong frames, needed filling out, though, he thought. Six husky, placid-faced, blue-eyed blond Russians standing in a row eyed Jancsi while he spoke to the guard who had brought them. The guard, a sullen man, looked up from the slip of paper Jancsi handed him.

"Where is this János Nagy who takes the prisoners?"

"I am János Nagy," said Jancsi.

The guard began to laugh. "Go wipe your nose, sonny. Where is your father? I have no time for jokes."

Jancsi faced him. He didn't seem angry, but his neck was set very straight in his shoulders. His arms moved back a little, ending in clenched fists.

"My father is in the war and I am doing his job. Take that back, about my nose, or . . . or I'll make you worry about your own."

"Well, I'll be . . ." the guard drew in his breath in surprise, eying Jancsi. "And I believe you would, too," he decided and began to laugh. "All right, young man. I take it back." He shrugged, handing Jancsi a small, flat key. "From now on you are responsible, not I. So long."

He mounted his waiting horse and rode away, leaving Jancsi with a small key he didn't know what to do with and six strange giants he didn't know what to do with, either. He looked at the key, wondering, when one of the prisoners grunted and five pairs of arms shot forward, chained together.

"Oooooh, the nasty brute!" Kate found her voice. "Take those chains off them this minute, Jancsi Nagy. The very idea!"

Uncle Moses had stepped out of the store. He looked worried but he gave Jancsi a smile. "I thought you could handle that fellow alone, but I was watching. Now that he is gone, bring these men into the store. I want to talk to you."

Jancsi was already fumbling with the lock on the chain. When it dropped into the dust, six pairs of blue eyes smiled at him and one prisoner poked a blunt finger at his chest.

"Comrade, eh? Friend?"

Jancsi nodded. "Sure. Friend."

Then Uncle Moses spoke to them in Russian and their faces lighted up still more. The six of them began to speak at once, surrounding the old man eagerly. After a while Uncle Moses emerged from the tight ring of blond giants around him.

"They like you, Jancsi. They say you must be a good farmer . . . the horses are so shiny." Cheerful as he sounded, his mind seemed to be on something else. He peered nervously up and down the long street. "Well, let's go inside," he said and herded the men ahead of him. The girls and Jancsi followed. Uncle Moses locked the door, then stood undecided, rubbing the end of his nose, peering now at Jancsi, then at the prisoners.

"You didn't see any gendarmes on the way, or did you, Jancsi?"

"No. Why?"

"This is a fine mess. I just don't know what to do," sighed Uncle Moses. "Peter deserted and the gendarmes are after him. I saw them. They say he was heading for home when last seen."

"Deserted!" breathed Jancsi. Kate and Lily drew closer. "Why?" They all knew that deserters were punished; it was the worst thing a soldier could do.

"Because old Vidor wrote him a letter and told him that Mari had a baby . . . and she isn't well. A foolish thing to do . . . worry a man about something he can't do anything about. Poor Peter, he is almost crazy."

"How do you know?" asked Jancsi, staring at Uncle Moses.

"Because he is here," sighed the old man, casting a glance at the small door in the rear. The six prisoners sat immobile on the boxes and crates, great hands spread on much-mended knees, looking uncomprehending but content from one speaker to another. Somehow, perhaps because he didn't know what to say, Jancsi smiled at them. Six broad smiles answered. "Peter," said one of them, pointing to himself. "Grigori . . . Stana . . . Nicolai . . . Sergei . . ." and again "Peter" he pointed out one after another. Then he held up two fingers. "Peter, Peter," he grinned.

Jancsi nodded. "Jancsi," he said, tapping his chest. Then he turned to Uncle Moses. "They think we are talking about them. What will you do about our Peter?"

"All he wants is to see Mari and the baby. If I could get someone to drive him home . . . but every wagon going toward his home will be searched tonight, every road watched. And if they find him here, it's court martial for both of us."

They looked at each other helplessly. Suddenly Kate exclaimed: "I have an idea! Listen. Lily and I will take the wagon, get Mari and the baby, and come back here. Then we'll hide Peter under our skirts and go home. They wouldn't watch wagons going to our farm. Why should they?"

"How about these?" asked Jancsi. "Will they fly home . . . or what?"

"Oh," said Kate, deflated, staring at the prisoners. "I . . . I forgot about them."

Grigori, Stana, Nicolai, Sergei, and the two Peters beamed at her. "Ho! Dushinka." "Why don't you tell them, Uncle

Moses?" said Lily. "Look at them. They are nice. Let's do what Kate said, then we can all drive home, prisoners and all." Her voice grew more and more eager, then she burst out laughing. "Those gendarmes wouldn't even dream that Kate, Mari, the baby, Lily, Jancsi, Grigori, Nicolai, Stana, Sergei, and two Peters are sitting on top of the third one!"

Jancsi sat up straight. "Not bad. You know, I am beginning to believe that you two have brains. What do you say, Uncle Moses?"

Uncle Moses was rubbing his nose in earnest and that meant that he was thinking hard. "If we can get away with it, Peter could steal away, back to the front, much easier from your farm. They only watch soldiers coming away. Going back, he could join all the others. Jancsi, it's an awful risk but . . ."

"But somebody left another pack of trouble on your doorstep and this time, *this* time we are going to cart it away," said Jancsi resolutely. Kate and Lily jumped up. "Let's go!"

"My eggs!" cried Uncle Moses. He spoke rapidly to the Russians and unlocked the door. The six giants goosefiled out and came back, each carrying a basket of eggs.

"*Jajca*," Nicolai sighed, caressing the basket with his eyes.

"Give them some, Uncle Moses. They look hungry," said Kate from the door. "And here . . . you ask them . . . ask them if they have seen Daddy."

Then the wagon rattled away. Uncle Moses locked the door again. He tapped lightly on the rear door and after a moment Aunt Sarah emerged.

"How is he?" asked Uncle Moses.

"Asleep," she smiled. "He was starved and dead on his feet. Ten days since he had warm food or more than a few minutes' rest. Hunted like a poor rabbit. . . ." She broke off as she became aware of the big shadowy shapes.

"It's all right, Mama. Jancsi's prisoners. Six more for you to feed . . . if you can manage?" She only nodded smiling reassurance and was gone.

Uncle Moses began to speak to the prisoners. As he talked and they began to understand what was happening, those broad, placid faces became windows through which Jancsi could see their thoughts. First slow comprehension tinged with amusement, then compassion, and finally approval and admiration. They smiled at him; they nodded vigorously, repeating: "Comrade . . . comrade." To Uncle Moses they talked eagerly, once in a while touching his hand, his arm, with clumsy but gentle appeals for more attention. Uncle Moses translated small shreds of the stories they were pouring into his ears.

"Grigori has a baby daughter he has never seen yet. Nicolai has a small farm and ten children. . . . Sergei says you are a brave boy, Jancsi; he has one about your age. . . . No, none of them knew Kate's father . . . of course not. They haven't been home since the war began."

All talk ceased suddenly as Aunt Sarah appeared with a huge steaming pot and a handful of spoons. "Ho!" the Russians grunted as one man and fell to, not waiting for the forthcoming plates, kneeling on the floor around the pot.

"Muzhiks, small farmers, all of them. They don't know

what it's all about; they only want to go home," sighed Uncle Moses.

Night was falling. The little store was dark when the wagon pulled up and Kate pounded on the door. "Hurry!" she panted, slipping inside. "The gendarmes are searching the houses up above. They stopped us both coming and going, but they don't know who Mari is. We brought the cow too, she wouldn't leave the brown cow." For a moment her gay smile rested on Jancsi, then: "Hurry, please."

Jancsi gasped when Uncle Moses led the staggering, trembling Peter from the store-room. This hollow-eyed, shivering wreck with the unkempt beard, could this be Peter? The Russians surrounded and almost carried him to the wagon. Mari was sobbing softly, but she didn't cry out. Lily took the baby from her and Mari cradled her husband's head on her lap. One by one Grigori, Stana, Nicolai, Sergei, and the two Peters climbed in, hiding the third Peter completely. Jancsi threw a horse-blanket over their knees, then jumped up to the seat.

"God bless you, children," said Uncle Moses hoarsely as the wagon moved away. They traveled slowly because of Mari's cow tied behind. At the beginning of the lane one of the horses snorted and an answering snort came from behind the trees. A moment later a voice said: "Stop," and two gendarmes rode into the light cast by the wagon lanterns.

"Where are you going?" demanded one of them.

"Home," said Jancsi quietly although his heart was pounding in his throat. He fished a piece of paper out of his pocket.

"Here. Government order. I am taking prisoners home for fieldwork."

"Six prisoners . . . János Nagy," the gendarme mumbled. "That seems to be in order. The big ranch we have just come from." He jerked a thumb behind him as an explanation to his partner. He returned the paper to Jancsi. "Your mother said you'd be along with them and two girls." His eyes explored the wagon casually.

Jancsi forestalled a question. "We are taking Mari . . . Mari Vidor and her baby home. She is sick. Her husband is in the war."

"You Mari Vidor?" asked the gendarme, peering at Mari. She nodded, tears streaming down her deathly pale face. The stern eyes of the gendarme softened. "Don't worry, Sister. He'll be home before you know it. Little tyke," he smiled at the baby, tickling her under the chin until she gurgled. "Does he know about this?" He winked at Mari. She, almost fainting with terror least Peter make a move, began to sob.

"Don't cry, Sister; we are all in the same mess," the gendarme grunted. "We have to hunt for a man tonight, God forgive us. I don't want to find him, but orders is orders. He deserted to see his wife. Peter Hódi. You know him?" he turned to Jancsi.

"Sure. But he lives three miles the other side of the village."

"I know. Those roads are watched and if he tries . . ." Something like a groan escaped him. "Son, it's a crazy world when it's a man's duty to kill, and a sin to comfort his wife. Well," he sighed, "go on home."

The shadows swallowed him up and Jancsi clucked to the horses. He felt weak and his teeth were chattering now that the danger was over. Behind him a soft Russian voice broke the silence: "Comrade . . ."

He turned around, but Grigori wasn't talking to him. He was holding out his big arms for Mari's baby and she gave it to him. Grigori began to croon, then Stana, Nicolai, Sergei, and the two Peters began to hum too. And the wagon swayed on homeward with six big Russians singing a lullaby to a small Hungarian baby.

CHAPTER VIII

JUST CAME

PETER stayed at the farm for a week, just long enough to regain his strength. He seemed relieved of his worry, for Mother had assured him that his wife and baby Panni could stay with them as long as Mari wished. Mari's parents, the old Vidors, were too poor now to take on an extra burden and Peter's farm, no matter how small, was too large a task for Mari to run alone.

He left as stealthily as he had come, and a week later a small pink card proclaimed that he had fared well. Mother was reading the card over Mari's shoulder, stroking her hair.

"You see, Mari dear, he is all right. Now you can smile again and get well."

161

"He will never be all right again Mrs. Nagy," whispered Mari, reaching for Mother's hand.

"This man . . . he was not my Peter. He was a stranger I don't know and, God forgive me, I cannot love."

"Mari, Mari, don't say that. He was only tired and discouraged," Mother comforted her, knowing even while she spoke that Mari was right. Much more was wrong with Peter than exhaustion and discouragement. There was hatred in Peter's heart, lashing out blindly at everything that seemed half secure in this war-torn country.

"*You* are safe, what are *you* worrying about?" Peter had glowered at her. "Mr. Nagy has enough money to buy himself a nice, soft spot somewhere behind the trenches. After the war he will come home, the *hero,* and make slaves of us again. Ride around on his fine horse while we do the work . . . *we,* the peasants!"

"Peter!" Jancsi had cried out, his face white from the shock. "You can say *that* about my father?"

"Yes, and about that fine friend of yours too . . . that Jew. I wish he had left me alone. I don't want favors from him. The profiteer . . . growing fat and rich on us! The old spider. Sitting in his store, waiting for the money we have earned!"

Jancsi would have hit him then, but for the long look Mother gave him. That look, so gentle, so full of pity, had arrested his hand and sealed his lips.

"You don't know what you are saying, Peter," sighed Mother. "Uncle Moses has been like a good father to the whole village. Ask anyone. . . ."

"I don't have to ask!" shouted Peter. "I know what the soldiers are saying at the front. He is no Uncle Moses to me! They make a profit on all of us while we fight for them. . . ."

Mother took Jancsi's arm then and they left the room. They didn't speak; what was there to say? Something, somebody had poisoned Peter's soul against those who had been good to him all his life. Into Jancsi's mind flashed the words Father had said: "The stampede . . . the mad whirlwind that sucks in men . . . and spits out crippled wrecks." Crippled in body and soul, Jancsi thought then, with an understanding far beyond his years.

"Poor Peter," he said aloud. Mother pressed his arm. "I knew you would see it that way, Son. I only hope the war ends before this poison has spread too far. But look," she smiled then, "one of your bears wants something."

She had called the Russians "bears" since first she laid eyes on them. They followed Jancsi around, tramping behind him in their big, clumsy boots, trying to understanding what he was saying. Uncle Moses was right, though. The horses and farm-tools, the cows, chickens, and sheep, formed the first link of understanding. A few weeks after they had come, they knew the Hungarian words for everyday things all around the ranch and from then on they learned very fast. When the sheep were driven in for winter quarters, Jancsi tried to show them how the feeding troughs and water fountains were arranged. Grigori—he seemed to be the boss—calmly pushed him aside. "Me do," he said, and in no time the folds were in order.

"Me do," became a byword on the farm. Haul in wood and

chop it? "Me do," Nicolai would say. Feed and clean animals?
"Me do," and Sergei sprang into action. Milk the cows? "Me
do," Stana had declared soon after the plowing was done, and
"Me do" it was from then on. Grigori had taken charge of
baby Panni with such determination that Mari surrendered
the child to him the moment he appeared, face and hands
scrubbed red, a large apron of Mother's tied around him. His
clumsy, callused hands became light, gentle, as if he were holding a fragile flower. Big Peter and Bigger Peter, as the family
had labeled the two Russian Peters, had been shepherds in
Russia. They lived and slept in the fields, leaving their charges
only long enough to eat their meals.

The only person who held out against the authoritative "Me
do" of Grigori was Kate. Her chickens were *her* chickens and
that was all there was to that.

"You are a nice Russian, Grigori," she said to him one day,
"but leave my chickens alone. You don't know anything
about chicken raising."

"Ho! Grigori know chicken. Grigori do," he laughed.

"Oh, no, you won't! These are not Russian chickens."

"Ho! Chicken is chicken." But Kate stamped her foot. "No.
Me do. Go away!"

Grigori went, laughing. From the yard he turned back.
"Ho! Chicken is chicken . . . little devil is little devil, Russko,
Magyarsko . . . all same!"

It was Sergei who adopted Jancsi. He managed to be always
in sight, following him with his eyes, listening to every word
he said. When in early December the first heavy snow fell,

Sergei began to look worried. One day he shuffled and clumped around Jancsi, taking everything Jancsi started to do, right out of his hands.

"What's the matter with you, Sergei?" laughed Jancsi. "Can't I even wash my own face without you handing me a towel?"

This was too long a sentence for Sergei. He shook his head, then waved his arm around. "Snow."

"That's right, snow."

"No much work now," said Sergei, looking anxiously at Jancsi's face.

"There is enough."

Sergei shook his head sadly. "No much work now. Jancsi send Russian back to camp. . . ."

"Oh!" Jancsi understood now what had worried Sergei. He thumped him on the back. "No, no. Jancsi *like* Russian. Jancsi *keep* Russian. Don't you worry, Sergei!"

"Ho, ho, HO!" Sergei was shouting, his face a sudden sunbeam of a grin. He ran into the yard.

"Grigori, Stana, Nicolai, Peter, Peter," he bellowed and they came tramping through the snow. "Jancsi *like* Russian, Jancsi *keep* Russian!" he announced, beaming around the circle of questioning faces. His shouts had brought the whole family out and suddenly they all found themselves hugged and kissed soundly. Grigori picked Kate and Lily right off their feet and was dancing around, holding them on his arms as if they had been feathers.

"My saints!" gasped Kate after they calmed down a little. "What's got into them?"

Grigori was holding Jancsi by the arm. "Jancsi . . . hear," he began, struggling with words still strange to him. "Look, see"—he pointed to the snow-covered plains—"see, steppe . . . like Russia. Good." He turned to the group. "Mother . . . like Mamushka. Good. Baby . . . Jancsi . . . work . . . horse . . . cow . . . all same. Good." He frowned, at loss for words to express what was really on his mind. Then he laid a big hand on Jancsi's heart. "In here, all same. Good. *Good*."

A grin spread over his solemn face. "More." He looked at Kate. "Chicken . . . all same. Little devil . . . all same. Grigori *like*."

Kate marched up to him. "Me do," she grinned and, standing on tiptoe, gave him a resounding kiss.

And so when Christmas came, the walls of the old kitchen embraced a large family again. The shepherds who brought in a new lamb for the baby were clad in drab remains of an enemy's uniform; the songs the men sang were strange tunes born on the Russian steppes; somewhere in the winter night guns were roaring; but here in the old kitchen peace still reigned and good will among men.

The day after Christmas the second snowstorm came. It lasted for a week and it was two more weeks before enough of it had melted and blown away so Jancsi could ride to the village for mail. He tramped into the store, cheeks aglow with the wind and anticipation. "Will I need a bag, Uncle Moses?" he said, holding out both hands.

Even Uncle Moses couldn't find a way to soften the blow of an empty pigeonhole. He was too wise to say meaningless words about the storm and delay; he had seen that Jancsi's eyes had already taken in the stacks of pink cards waiting for others.

Finally it was sturdy Jancsi who found a crutch of a thought to lean on. "Father is all right or somebody else would have written. We would have heard. . . ."

As weeks went by, growing into months, and he had to go home each time without news from Father, he came to dread the moment when Mother's anxious face would appear in the doorway and he had to snuff out the tiny flame of hope in her eyes. She was so brave. Somehow she would summon a smile and say: "No news is good news, Son. Let's read the book and see what he wants us to do."

The book had become a tower of strength for them. It was part of Father, and even if they knew every word of it by heart, reading it brought Father into the old kitchen.

Even the Russians knew about it. Grigori would come in every morning. "What big boss say today, Jancsi? Go read." He would nod approval of every word. "Big boss good man. He think good things to do." And he saw to it that every wish of a man unknown to him was carried out. Two Peters took the sheep back to the pastures in April, and Nicolai seeded down the oatfields. Corn was planted in May, and potatoes. Young piglets grew round and pink under Sergei's careful hands. There were things Father couldn't foresee and those Grigori took upon himself. Baby Panni had grown as round and pink as the piglets but she could squeal much louder. She had learned that a full-throated yell would bring

"Big Gogi" running to pick her up and "Gogi" she loved. The only time she was really quiet was when Grigori played tunes to her on a small balalaika he had fashioned from bits of wood and scraps of wire. Then they were both happy, gazing far, far away. Grigori was in Russia then, playing to his own baby daughter, and she in some fairyland.

"How these materials stretch!" sighed Mother one Sunday when she had dressed to go to church and the velvet bodice hung limp around her waist. Kate looked away quickly because her eyes had filled with tears and tears were forbidden in the house.

"If you have to bawl, go to the barn," said Jancsi to her one day, glaring. "If Mother can . . . if *she* doesn't cry, why should you?"

"I miss Uncle Márton . . . and Daddy," sobbed Kate, hurt.

"Go to the barn, then. That's where I go to . . . to miss them," said Jancsi, but now his voice was gentle.

June came again, still without news from Father. Then another blow fell. There was a letter in the mail from Mother's parents, whom Jancsi had never seen. They lived in the mountains close to the border and Mother had never had time to visit them since Jancsi was born and the old people were not to be coaxed away from their small farm. But now they had to leave it.

"Troops are marching through day and night," the letter said, "and even if we had food, we couldn't eat it. There are many far hungrier than we are. Could dear Márton come for us, Daughter? We have no other place to go. . . ."

Mother looked at Jancsi anxiously. "What will we do?"

"Go for them of course, and right away. Listen, Mother"—
he waved aside her "we can't leave the farm now"—"listen
to me. Grigori can run this place with both hands tied behind
his back. How far is that place?"

"Over fifty kilometers."

"Pff. I thought it was far. I can be home with Grandfather
and Grandmother in three days!"

"You are not going alone, Jancsi. I won't let you."

"Now, Mother."

But this time again Mother had her way. Jancsi had to take
Kate and Lily, because Mother wouldn't go, in case there
should be news from Father. Mari couldn't go with the baby
and that left Jancsi with the two girls to take whether he
wanted to or not.

So Grigori had his way after all; he was to take care of
Kate's chickens. He listened solemnly to the endless instruc-
tions Kate gave him. "Me know. Me do."

"Me know . . . me know!" cried Kate in exasperation. "All
right, Grigori. But if there is *one* dead chicken here when I
come back, there'll be a dead Russian!"

Grigori laughed. "Me know. No dead chicken . . . no dead
Russian. Me do."

Two days later they started off. The wagon was loaded with
enough food to last them a month. Uncle Moses had given
Jancsi a map and explained over and over again how to follow
it. He gave Jancsi letters to friends who lived on the way,
with whom they could stay. "With a little luck you won't

have to stop but once for overnight. At Abel Blum's. Your horses should be able to travel twenty-five kilometers in a day, easily."

Mother of course was full of last-minute misgivings and, had Jancsi listened to her, the whole expedition would have been called off. Only this time he didn't listen, but sat stony-faced and patient until Mother ran out of words. Then he came to life. "Yes, Mother. See you in three days from now," and cracked his whip over the horses.

Over the road between the grainfields, across the ferry, past the corrals, and then into the mountains they went. Neither of them had ever been farther north than the corrals; now new scenery opened before their eyes at every turn of the road, which cut through forests, passed small villages and towns, going uphill nearly all the time.

"Beautiful, isn't it!" exclaimed Lily when the road swung around the side of a wooded mountain and the whole world seemed to be spread out below them. Houses were tiny white dots on the green slopes, villages no more than a cluster of white. The river wound its blue, shimmering way around hills and clumps of trees and on the horizon stretched the towering line of the Carpathian Mountains.

Jancsi, while he had to admit that it was beautiful to look at from where they were, heartily disapproved of the idea of living in a place like this. "Imagine trying to plow one of those awry fields. Or having mountains look in your window all the time. Not for me! Bad for the horses too. Up and down, up and down all the time."

The horses didn't seem to mind, but went along contentedly. When noon came they found themselves near the village Uncle Moses had marked on the map with one word: EAT. They rested and ate in the shade of a tremendous oak tree, close to a clear, chattering brook. Kate filled the jugs with fresh water, then they started up again. In spite of Jancsi's grumbling, the road persisted in going up . . . and up . . . and up. When sunset came, the sun was far below them and haze covered the valleys with purple veils. Ahead, lights began to twinkle, then they were driving down a strange street.

Jancsi stopped at a small, homy-looking store to ask where Abel Blum lived. He didn't realize how tired he was until his feet were on the ground. Tired and very sleepy. Kate and Lily had fallen asleep long ago. "A lot of help they are!" he grumbled and walked into the store.

"I am Abel Blum," said the tall, aging man, taking the letter Jancsi pushed under his eyes by way of inquiry. He looked remotely like Uncle Moses only he was much taller and not so old. Jancsi studied his face while he scanned the letter, then studied the store. It was very much like Uncle Mo's, it even smelled the same, a little bit of everything but mostly cheese.

It must have been a long letter, but finally Mr. Blum looked up. "Now I know a lot about you, Jancsi, and I can see that you are very tired. It must have been quite a journey."

"It was nothing," said Jancsi modestly, but he had to yawn.

"Well, bring the girls in. I'll take care of the horses later," said Mr. Blum.

Jancsi sighed with relief. Mr. Blum was truly like Uncle Moses; he didn't fuss, simply got down to business.

When Jancsi came back with the stumbling, yawning girls, Mr. Blum's wife was in the store, reading the letter. "Such babies," she smiled, putting her arms around them. She must have seen the fleeting frown on Jancsi's face because she added quickly: "Not you, Jancsi. It takes a man to do what you are doing."

She led them into a small, cheerful kitchen behind the store and fed them. Food smelled and tasted good but it didn't interest the three tired travelers half so much as the prospect of bed. She knew it too, because soon they were stumbling up narrow stairs behind her friendly candle and then there was only friendly darkness and sleep.

"They are so nice," smiled Lily next morning, when the wagon turned around a corner and they couldn't see the waving Blums any more. "I didn't even see them last night, I was so sleepy. That was a good breakfast too," she sighed contentedly.

"Was!" groaned Jancsi. "It still is, up to my neck. I ate enough to last me a week. I don't know what Grandfather was talking about . . . there seems to be plenty of food around." That night he knew that Grandfather didn't exaggerate. For in the afternoon the road they had to follow turned into the Army highway and the wagon became a small part of two unending streams of traffic flowing north and south. In the one going north they were almost the only travelers not in uniform. Jancsi had to keep to the very edge of the road because it was filled with a solid mass of marching soldiers. Often he had to stop and pull aside still further, to let roaring Army trucks by.

The stream going south was much thinner and slower. Peasant wagons, filled with the odds and ends of deserted homes, drawn by bony horses or oxen, driven by bony, lean men, crept along on it. Ambulances, long strings of them at a time, drove by. Groups of ragged soldiers with arms or heads bandaged tramped slowly along, and many of them sat by the roadside. Every time the wagon had to stop, there were some who pushed their way through the northward-marching columns, to turn haggard eyes on Jancsi. "Got any food, Son?" They had. Into every reaching hand Kate and Lily placed some part of the generous supply Mother had provided; lavishly first, then more and more sparingly. It couldn't last forever, no matter how much there was, and who knew how many more thin hands would reach out before the day was ended?

Jancsi had asked everyone: "Have you seen Corporal Márton Nagy of the Seventh Infantry? Or Major Béla Kormos?"

Only slowly shaking heads answered with a silent "No." And still he asked again and again until a wounded man laughed at him. "Son, did you ever try to find a needle in a haystack? Seventh Infantry! It was blasted to shreds in December. They are still picking up the pieces. . . ."

After that Jancsi didn't ask. He drove doggedly on and on, hard, burning eyes now on the road, now on the map spread on his knees. Somewhere along here they would cross and turn off the highway into a sideroad. That sideroad led straight to the hamlet where Grandfather lived, and Grandfather might have a barn into which he might creep later.

There was an Army hospital where the roads branched off; a whole city of low, gray-painted barracks. It was not marked on the map. The map was old, made in 1913, when the corner of the roads was a green field studded with white daisies and red poppies. Now it was 1916 and a hospital city sprawled on the corner. Flags fluttered on every building, white flags with red crosses.

Late afternoon found them in a narrow mountain lane to which kind strangers had directed Jancsi. At the end of the lane was the house where Mother was born. A poor little house, a few weedy slopes with corn struggling up between the weeds, and a tumbledown barn. That was all. But there were warm welcoming arms after the first surprise of the old people had worn off.

"We were expecting Daughter, or Márton! So you are Jancsi!" Grandfather held him at arm's length, joy shining in his eyes. "And little Kate! And who is the golden-haired child?"

Far into the night they talked and planned for tomorrow's journey home. A fat gray cat came in from the dark and made a beeline for Lily's lap.

"Scat!" cried Grandmother, flapping her hands. "Throw her down, child, she isn't our cat, she just came."

"Just came . . . from where?" asked Lily, cuddling the blissfully purring cat.

"Most of the neighbors have gone; one of them must have left her behind and she adopted us."

"Our livestock," chuckled Grandfather. "We ate the chickens, the soldiers ate the pigs, and now the cat is eating the rats that ate the corn."

"Take her with us tomorrow?" asked Lily.

"I wouldn't dream of it," said Grandmother with finality.

"Such a nice friendly cat you are, Just Came. You'll be lonesome if we, too, leave you behind," Lily crooned, her eyes hopefully on Grandmother.

"My dear child," she said, "these are no times to worry about a cat's feelings. You can see for yourself, if you hadn't saved some of the food you brought along, we would have gone to bed hungry."

"That's just it; what will she do?"

"Forage for herself in the woods," said Grandmother. When Lily hung her head, she went on, sadness creeping into her voice. "It isn't only this one cat, Lily. There are many homeless pets in the woods now, dogs and cats both. We have to harden our hearts, there is nothing else we can do. Listen." She lifted her hand. The silence was filled with a deep rumble.

"Thunder," said Kate.

"No, my dear. Those are the guns across the mountains. Every night we hear them and sometimes in the daytime when the wind blows from the north. Guns, little Lily, laughing at all human kindness. We can't worry about one stray cat."

She rose. "Put her out, child, then go to bed. This is where you and Kate will sleep."

By the dim light of one small candle she didn't notice that, while the door was opened and duly closed, no cat went out. A gray shadow, with tail waving in the air, followed Kate and Lily into the room. A wise little shadow who knew that she had found a friend.

"You didn't put her out," giggled Kate.

"And I'm not going to leave her behind, either. Listen, Kate, tomorrow . . ."

Whispers and suppressed giggles came from the bed, then silence. The cat jumped lightly onto the bed and settled down to a good wash. Maybe she knew that tomorrow she would be starting on a long journey.

If there was an extra basket which Kate and Lily had stowed under the seat, nobody noticed it in the excitement of leaving. And the basket didn't say anything for a long time. The wagon rattled down the mountain lane, through the hamlet, into the road, going down, down, down all the time. Grandmother's tears had dried and Grandfather had ceased to complain about the dust that made him blow his nose so often. Jancsi let him drive because he wanted to. He said he would like to look ahead instead of behind him and a team like this was the best start to look ahead to. They traveled slowly, but Jancsi didn't care. There was only one thought in his mind and he clung to that: "If anything has happened to Father, we would have heard." *We would have heard*, rattled the wheels. *We would have heard*, pounded the horses' feet.

By noon they were close to the Army highway. Jancsi watched the sprawling barracks of the hospital grow larger

as they approached the crossing and beyond he could see the endless streams pouring north and south.

"What was that?" Grandmother sat up with a start. A yowl, then another one came from under the seat. She looked at Lily, who was sitting as if she had swallowed a poker.

"You foolish child, you didn't . . ."

"Meow-ow-ow-oooow," answered the cat, dispelling all doubt. Grandmother looked at the guilty but triumphant faces of Kate and Lily. Her hands fluttered. "Well, what's done is done. You might as well give her air, wherever she is."

When the lid of the basket was lifted up, cautiously lest Just Came jump out, Lily began to wail. "She is sick . . . oh, look, Just Came is very sick."

Grandmother cast a glance into the basket. "She would pick out a time like this," she chuckled, then said to Lily: "Just leave her alone, she'll be all right. I knew we would have a handful if we didn't get rid of her."

"Meoooow-ow-ow," complained Just Came in answer.

"She isn't all right, either, shaking all over like that. Jancsi, Grandfather, please stop the wagon!" Lily cried. "I am taking her right straight to that hospital."

"Don't be funny, Lily," grumbled Jancsi. "Can't you see . . . ?"

"No, she can't and you ought to see that she can't," snapped Kate. "And I think we ought to take Just Came to the hospital too. Please."

"Meow, meoooow, meow-ow-ow. Please! Meow!!

Grandfather pulled over into the shade. "We might as well,

or we'll never hear the end of this rumpus," he sighed re-
signedly. "It's noontime, anyway."

"Coming, Jancsi?" asked Kate as she and Lily climbed off
the wagon.

"And have them in there laugh in my face? Oh, no. You
two started this; now you finish it. Girls! Humph!"

Kate shrugged. Carrying the noisy basket between them,
the two girls marched through the gate and into the nearest
barrack. A nurse stopped them at the door. "No visitors allowed, my dear. I'm sorry."

"We aren't visitors, we brought a patient. She needs a
doctor right away," cried Lily.

"She?" A doctor, on his way through the narrow hall, smiled
at Lily. "This is an Army hospital, child, for men. Wh—what
in the world . . . ?"

"Meeeow," came from the basket.

"Her," said Lily, opening the lid. "She won't mind the men."

"A cat! My saints!" exploded the doctor, staring at the
nurse, whose face was red from laughing.

"Is she . . . is she dying?" stammered Lily. "Oh, *please* do
something!"

"Well, now! Look here, my dear," said the doctor to Lily,
his face a mixture of mirth and annoyance. "Leave her in the
basket, here in the hall, go take a nice long walk, and by the
time you come back she'll be all right."

"Can't you give her a . . . pill or something?" wailed Lily.

"She won't need a pill; what she'll need is a larger basket," said
the doctor, who was already on his way again.

"What did he mean by that?" demanded Lily, her eyes growing round.

The nurse smiled. "Your cat is going to have kittens, dear, that's all."

"Kittens!" squealed Lily, beaming at Kate. Kate didn't seem very enthusiastic.

"Sure. A fine thing to happen on a trip like this, but, as Grandmother said, what's done is done."

"Do what the doctor said," smiled the nurse, "and in a little while you can take her home. I have to go to the ward now to feed the patients."

"Couldn't we help you instead of taking a walk?" asked Lily, all eagerness now.

'Well, now, I don't know why you couldn't," said the nurse after a moment's hesitation. "Come this way."

They entered the long ward. Two rows of beds stretched ahead on both sides, four long avenues of narrow white beds, close together. It was very quiet in the room.

"Take a bowl to each of the beds," the nurse instructed the girls. "If a man is asleep, don't disturb him. This is the convalescent ward," she explained, ladling soup from a caldron into bowls. "What they need is rest."

The ladle paused and she sighed wearily. "Rest. I have forgotten what rest means." She did look very tired. Kate took the ladle from her. "Let me do this. Lily can carry the bowls, you just sit here for a while."

The nurse sank into the chair with a grateful smile. "Thank you."

Almost an hour passed before all the patients had been fed. "There was only one asleep," Lily said, coming back with the empty bowls; "he even had the sheet pulled over his face."

The nurse followed Lily's pointing finger with her eyes. "Oh, the amnesia case. He sleeps most of the time."

"What's am—amnesia?" Kate wanted to know.

"Loss of memory. They forget who they are and have to begin life all over again; like babies."

"Does it hurt?"

"No," smiled the nurse. "It comes from a shock; like a big scare, you know." She looked toward the bed again. "He is such a nice man too, poor fellow. He tries so hard to remember. If we could find out who he is, find something to remind him of his home, he might remember. You want to see him?" she asked as Kate kept staring at the bed. "Come on then, but be quiet."

"No. 54, Amnesia," was written on the headboard. The nurse gently lifted the sheet. Pandemonium broke loose immediately. Kate, with her famous tin-whistle scream going at full blast, threw herself on the bed.

"UNCLE MARTON! UNCLE MAAARTON! It's KATE. Can't you . . . ? UNCLE MARTO-O-O-ON!"

Every patient was sitting bolt upright. Doctors and nurses were running in, Lily joined Kate, tugging at Uncle Márton's hands. "Say something . . . you know us, don't you? Say something."

"Kate, if you don't stop that infamous yelling this minute, I'll take Milky away from . . . Say! Where am I? Who are these people?" Uncle Márton was looking around dazedly.

"Never mind them," sobbed Kate, laughing at the same time. "You know who you are now, don't you?"

"Why shouldn't I? Let me out of this bed!" Uncle Márton cried, trying to peel Kate and Lily off his chest.

"Take it easy, take it easy," said a doctor who stepped up. "What is your name?"

"Lieutenant Márton Nagy of the Seventh Infantry," snapped Uncle Márton, glaring at him. "Seventh Infantry . . . Seventh . . . oh. . . ." His eyes clouded.

"Now it all comes back, doesn't it? You'll be all right now, Lieutenant Nagy. Don't think about that now. Tell me who this . . . this calliope is. That scream was the best I ever heard." The doctor sat down on the bed, smiling at Kate. "I wish we could produce one for each amnesia case we get; we wouldn't *have* any."

A new commotion started at the door and Jancsi's angry voice yelled: "Let me in! I tell you my cousin screamed. LET ME IN! You!! You hurt her and I'll . . ."

He burst through the crowd like a bombshell, then stood rooted to the ground. "Father." His lips formed the word but no sound came.

"Soldier! Forward, march!" said Father and held out his arms.

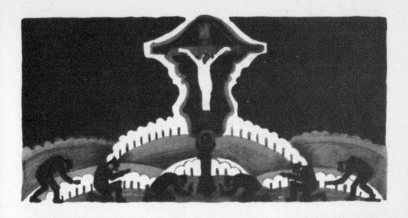

 CHAPTER IX

LIGHT A CANDLE

FATHER was home; home for at least six months but possibly more, as the doctors had said. By that time the war might be over. Just might, because Serbia was conquered, the huge Russian Army on the run, and the holocaust that shook France, Belgium, and Italy seemed very far away from the sun-drenched farm.

The children and the doctor had become great friends. First it looked as if they would have to leave Father in the hospital until mysterious items such as "identification papers," "leave of absence," and other tongue-twisting nonsense as far as Jancsi was concerned, could be arranged. But Kate showed all the signs of producing another hair-raising trumpet call, Grandmother declared that Just Came was really the finger of Destiny for producing five kittens practically on the bed of a missing man, and only fools would battle against Destiny. The doctor, she said, didn't look like a fool, so surely he could do something to let Father go home. Besides, Just Came and the five little Just Cames would need a lot of milk, and was the doctor going to rob sick men of precious milk to feed it to a bunch of no good cats? She took back the "no good" at a glance from Lily.

"All right, child. My old ears have been deafened by the guns; I couldn't hear the weak call of a cat for a little kindness. We can thank you for sharp ears and a pitying heart."

The doctor smiled then. "Thank Just Came. She had it all planned. Look at her! She is laughing at us, poor humans, who cannot see in the dark."

They stood around the large basket the nurse had found, admiring Just Came. She looked back at them through eyes half closed with bliss, kneading the bed of surgical dressing. Five tiny blind mites of nondescript color swarmed around her, not at all aware of the ring of giants surrounding their nest, and not giving a hoot about the wonderful part they had played in some human's life.

"One family of cats will never have to worry about a good home again, I can see that!" chuckled the doctor.

"These?" cried Jancsi. "They can have a . . . *bath* in milk every day if they want to. I'd even milk a special cow for them myself!"

"You come with me, Jancsi," said the doctor then. "We'll see the little chiefs and the big chief. You tell them about your father, the farm, the cats, and everything and maybe . . . just maybe they'll let you take Father home."

There was more to it than that, though. The doctor had to produce charts and X-rays to prove that Father was all right, then there was a delay until telegrams and telephone calls proved that Father was really the one he said he was. Plain foolishness, thought Jancsi. Couldn't they *see* that Father was all right and did they think he would *lie?*

But by next morning everything had been arranged, even to a borrowed lieutenant's uniform for Father. "From Corporal to Lieutenant in a year. Pretty good, Lieutenant Nagy," an officer with a lot of gold braid all over him said to Father. "And a handful of medals to catch up with you, as I heard. What did you do?"

Father looked him straight in the eye. The muscles in his jaws were working. "I don't know, sir. I would rather not try to remember."

The officer sighed. "Go home, Lieutenant. Forget, if you can. I wish I could."

It was late evening when the wagon turned the last turn in the road leading home. The house glowed with candlelight. Father said in a husky voice:

"You children drive to the barn and don't you dare come to the house before I call you. Understand? Grandpa, Grandma, and I will walk in."

"Yes, sir."

The three dogs barked like mad, suddenly stopped, and whined their welcome. The children waited in the dark until the door opened and closed, then Jancsi said, clucking to the horses: "He didn't want us to see them cry. I know." He knew. Didn't joy and happiness make a baby out of him in that hospital?

Grigori was the first to welcome them in the barn. Blinking, because he had fallen asleep in the hay, the first words he said were: "No dead chicken . . . no dead Russian."

Kate, Lily, and Jancsi, talking all at once, tried to tell him the great news. All he could understand for a while was the basket of cats. "Ho! Li'l' cat," he grinned, holding up five fingers. "Mamushka cat—Grigori. Li'l' cat—Peter, Nicolai, Sergei . . ."

"Listen, Grigori!" Jancsi tugged at him. "Big boss here. Big boss home. Understand?" Grigori's mouth fell open. "Big boss home? HO! Hoooo! Stana, Nicolai, Sergei, Peter, Peter . . . come!" he bellowed and Russians swarmed in from the dark. "Jancsi say big boss home."

"Good?" they questioned Jancsi. "All good? Leg, arm, head, belly—all good?"

"Yes, yes."

"Me go see!" Grigori lunged to the barn door, but Jancsi held him back. "Not now. He is in the house with Mother."

"Ho," nodded the six Russians understandingly. "Mamushka cry. Big boss cry. All same . . . Russko, Magyarsko. Sad? No cry. Happy? Cry. All same."

There was a little silence while the six Russians looked into the future and saw themselves going home. Grigori smiled at what he saw. "Sure. Grigori big man . . . Grigori bawl like . . . like *cow* when he see Russian Mamushka."

"Like a bull, Grigori," giggled Kate.

"Ho! Cow, bull, big like Grigori. Bawl all same." Then he winked ponderously at Kate. "Chicken make much egg for Grigori. Me do all time now?"

"All right," sighed Kate. "You take care of the chickens and I'll make new shirts for all of you."

"Plenty pretty flower on shirt? Like Russia?"

"Yes, yes. Only these will be Hungarian flowers on the shirts. I know, I know," she laughed when Grigori opened his mouth. "All same, Russko, Magyarsko."

"Sure. All same." The six Russians nodded happily.

They couldn't do enough for Father from that first night on. They welcomed him like a long-lost friend, pounding him on the back, and exploring him for injuries with clumsy fingers, until one of them noticed the gold star on his collar.

"Ho. Officer!" Sergei exclaimed and all of them stood at attention. Father laughed.

"Listen, men. I am a farmer. You are farmers. We are . . ."

"All same," giggled Kate, but Grigori shook his head.

"No all same, little devil. He big boss. He good man, write good book. Grigori, Sergei, Nicolai, Stana, Peter, Peter do what big boss say. Little devil do same, little devil grow big *faaat* Mamushka. Little devil no do same, she be dead little devil. Grigori do."

Kate laughed. "I'll take the chickens away from you if you talk like that."

But Grigori had other ideas. He put his hand to his ear and grinned at Father. "Big boss hear little noise? Big boss say: Grigori do chicken, Grigori do. Big boss say: Grigori jump in well, Grigori jump. Little devil make noise, Grigori no hear."

And that was that. Even Jancsi couldn't give them orders. "You li'l' boy now, Jancsi." Sergei waved him aside. "Go play. Big boss away, you work."

"He won't go away for a long time, Sergei," beamed Jancsi. "The doctor said he needed rest. After Christmas he will have to report to the hospital, but by that time the war will be over."

"Huh. Maybe," grunted Sergei, not very reassuringly. "Go play, Jancsi. You li'l' boy for li'l' time now."

So Jancsi had time to take long rides to the corrals, plan for new foals with old Arpád, tramp to the brook with the girls to pick flowers, romp with the dogs and the cats. He was a boy again, not because Sergei ordered him to be, but because a miracle had brought Father home whole, unharmed, and given Jancsi a little time to be what he was: a fifteen-year-old child.

Father never spoke of the war and soon they all learned not to ask about it, because then his face would darken as if he were in pain. Once in a while he told small, poignant stories, but there were no cannon belching death or wounded screaming for mercy in the memories he shared with his family. He

spoke of the small bird with the broken wing one of the men had picked up, and how the little bird had become tame during the weeks its wing was healing; how they had let it go on a September morning and how it sang to them before it soared away. About lone dogs guarding ruins of houses, and of cats waiting for a door to open that had no walls around it.

Into the quiet pool of respite from worry, dropped news from outside—Rumania entering the war in August, the death of the old Emperor Francis Joseph in November—as withered leaves drop into a pond, causing hardly a ripple.

Christmas came again. The kitchen door was open on Christmas Eve for the Christ Child, who had already brought precious gifts. Lily's father was home on leave and brought his frail wife to the farm for a few days. There was a long letter from Uncle Sándor, written in August, to be sure, but it had come the day before Christmas. There was a photograph in it of himself with a Russian family. He was standing behind a softly smiling tall girl and underneath he had written: "Sonia. She is very kind. She sends her love to a little devil who loves Russians."

There were gifts for everyone under the tree. Grigori, Stana, Nicolai, Sergei, and the two Peters couldn't wait for Christmas Day to put on the embroidered shirts Kate and Lily had made for them. They tore out to the barn with their packages and strutted back all dressed. Then they proceeded to kiss the whole gathering, including Major Kormos and Father.

"Stick those shirt-tails into your trousers, Grigori," laughed Kate. "Those are Hungarian shirts."

"Maybe. Pants Russian pants. No can stick shirt-tail in Russian pants," Grigori protested.

Father had saved one story for Christmas Eve and told it while the candles were burning on the tree. The faint sound of village church-bells coming across the plains made his story of another Christmas Eve sound like a song of hope, hope that maybe kindness and love of peace would be strong enough to stop the war soon. For the first time he spoke of things like offensive, march, trenches, shellfire, but the dark picture these words created was only a backdrop against which his story of human souls shone all the brighter.

"Last Christmas Eve," he began, "we had received orders to be prepared for a surprise attack against the Russians. Our trenches had been under heavy fire for days; we had either to retreat or to advance, and those who plan the moves of war decided on an advance.

"We had been waiting for hours, crouching against the walls of our trenches, when the word came: 'Go.'

"We crept out into the snow, countless silent dark shapes against the whiteness, and ran to the sunken road which lay between our lines and the mountainside where the Russian trenches were. Shells screamed overhead and burst behind us, drowning out all noise we might have made, and when we reached the road, whispered orders from the Captain scurried down the line like mice: 'Advance along the road. Don't dare make a sound or strike a light.'

"We tramped in knee-deep snow, skirting the friendly hillside that sheltered us from the fire, stealing toward the Russians. And then, just ahead of me I saw a boy kneel in the snow before a wayside crucifix and light a candle. It flickered in the still air, casting a feeble light on the image of Christ above it. 'Oh, Lord,' the man next to me sighed, reaching into his knapsack for a candle. Others had seen the glowing light, and as I looked around I saw that more and more candles were lighted all around. A whisper spread, like the order from the Captain from mouth to mouth, only this was not an order from the Captain. 'Light a candle for Christmas Eve,' men whispered and their very words seemed to turn into tiny stars as dozens and dozens, then hundreds of candles came forth from the knapsacks to be lighted and stuck in the snow. The hillside now was one glow of light and the crucifix was bright with an unearthly brightness. We were a target for the Russian guns, but we never gave it a thought. For a little while we were lost in prayer, until one of the men cried: 'They have stopped firing. Look!'

"Across the valley, on the hillside where the Russians were entrenched, a few small flames began to tremble, then more and more. Candles, hundreds of them, thousands, one for every gun that now was silent. Around me men began to sing 'Holy Night, Silent Night,' and from across the valley the song came back to us a thousandfold. Behind the lines so facing each other, the guns had ceased to roar and no more shells were screaming between men and the stars. Perhaps the Christ Child had walked between the lines and while He walked, peace had stayed the guns."

Father had finished his story. Lily's mother held out her

hand to him. "Thank you, Márton. I'll never forget this night."

Kate sighed, a long, tremulous sigh: "Oh, that was beautiful! What happened after?" Father shivered as if with the cold and rose to close the door. Only then did he answer:

"The candles burned down, Kate, and . . . darkness closed in again. Let those who made the war hear the story of what happened after. Let them see. . . ." He lifted his arm and covered his eyes, but when he looked up his face was smiling. "Oh, no. This is another Christmas Eve, and the Christ Child must not find hate in our hearts. Only pity for those who are responsible, for there is no man on earth wicked enough to have knowingly unleashed this power of darkness upon mankind."

Knowingly, no. But it was loose, this power called the war, and while it was roaming the earth no one could hold peace and happiness for long. It still demanded heartbreak and tears and helpless suffering from all those whose lives it couldn't take.

Lily's father had had to leave soon after Christmas but her mother stayed on. She said that all the doctors and nurses in the hospital had not done her as much good as a week on this peaceful farm.

"Stay here with us, then!" cried Mother.

"Yes, I would like to. I felt that I was coming home when I first saw the lighted windows from the lane. The very trees on the lane seemed to whisper: 'Come. We will lead you home.' "

Then Father went to report to the hospital and this time Mother and Jancsi went with him. The doctors found that in body he was sound, but only time, long months or even years, could make him forget the things he never spoke about.

"There are none braver than he is," the doctor told Mother, "but the human mind can stand just so much of horror and no more. We dare not take the risk of sending him back to war."

"Thank God!" Mother had exclaimed, and the doctor smiled very sadly.

"I hear that every day now. Wives, mothers thanking the Lord for an injury their beloved ones have received. A broken bone, a brave mind darkened with nameless fear, anything that takes a long time to heal, has become a blessing, a gift. They are safe for a little while longer."

"Big boss come home . . . maybe war over?" Grigori wanted to know when they had come home with Father. Jancsi tried to explain and he thought that Grigori didn't understand because for a long while he didn't say anything. Then he sighed: "Grigori know. Hear, Jancsi. Bad man, stupid man, he go kill and laugh. Good man, man with good heart, good head, no can kill and laugh. He cry inside. Baby cry with big noise. Man cry—no noise, but it hurt very bad. Me know . . . me know."

More white envelopes were coming to the village now than ever since the war started. The hands of Uncle Moses began to tremble and he seemed to grow smaller, more bent. Aunt Sarah was like a silent little wraith, going from house to house to comfort, to help, or just sit, holding the hand of a woman who would never wait for the mail again because there was no one left to write to her. Often she and the priest met in one of the houses and the priest would bow deeply to her. Once he told Father: "She seems to give more comfort, more strength to these poor women than I can."

No one knew that one white envelope had found its way to the little store, until one day in March Jancsi asked: "Uncle Mo, you haven't told me anything about Aaron and Dr. Sam. How are they?"

Uncle Moses smiled, a smile bleaker than pale winter sunlight trembling on snow. "They are both well, thank you, Jancsi. Aaron is coming home on leave in April and Sam has gone to Joseph. Two weeks ago."

"Uncle Mo," stammered Jancsi, searching for words and finding none, but Uncle Moses began to shuffle some papers. He held a newspaper out to Jancsi. "Take this home, Jancsi. There is something in here that will interest your father. I marked it."

"Yes, Uncle Mo," whispered Jancsi, who had learned that there are hurts so deep that one cannot reach them or heal them with words. He had to leave Uncle Moses with the wintry little smile and trembling hands, staring at nothing in the dark store.

"At nothing, Mother," he sobbed against her heart and she stroked his head.

"No, Son. He was just looking at things that might have been, but for the war. He is the strongest man I know."

Father spoke from behind the paper: "He is not looking back, but ahead. That makes him strong. Thinking of the living, not the dead. Look what he has sent me."

The article Uncle Moses had sent was one about the blockade against Germany. France and England had closed all the roads on land and sea which might carry food to Germany. They were being starved into defeat, and German children were without milk or any nourishing food. The Hungarian Government issued a plea to farmers, to take children—as many as they could feed—children, who were the most helpless of sufferers in the war.

Father looked up at Mother's face. "We have a large house," he said, but it sounded like a question. She smiled. "And a small family? I remember, Márton. But now we have a large house and a large family and it will be still larger. I would feed an army of hungry children . . . if we could."

"Let's start with five. That's a lucky number." He smiled at Lily. "Five blind kittens have found me; we will give each of them a child to play with."

Mother began to laugh. "Just Came is ahead of you, Márton. There are six more in the hayloft."

"All spoken for," Jancsi announced, smiling. "If Just Came has fifty kittens, they will all have homes. Every child in the village wants one of the lucky kittens to"—his face saddened—"to find their fathers for them. Some of them don't even know. . . ."

Father broke in, his face, too, dark with pain: "Five children, then, Mother? Little towheaded Germans?"

"Six, Márton, please. One for each kitten and one for baby Panni."

"That makes . . . how many additions to a small family of three? Let's count. Begin with Kate." Father was smiling again.

"Kate, Sándor, Lily, her mother now, Grigori, Sergei, Nicolai, Stana, Peter, Peter, Mari, baby Panni, Grandma, Grandpa, and six little towheaded Germans to come. Twenty!" cried Mother, throwing up her hands.

"Don't forget the three dogs and I don't know how many kittens," grinned Jancsi.

"Well," Father sighed. "Quite a houseful. Well, we have been blessed with a home that can take care of them. Tomorrow I shall ride into town with Jancsi and make out the papers."

Once again in the Town Hall of the same railroad town, father and son bent over long sheets of paper.

"Get . . . get a boy or two, Father, please . . . if you can. There are too many women on the place."

"How about the Russians?" laughed Father.

"They . . . they aren't boys. It would be nice to . . . to show a boy my herd and maybe teach him to ride. He could help me to break in my horses. . . ."

"How old?" asked Father, holding his pen over the line: "State age preferred."

"My age. No, a little younger. A boy like I was three years ago. Fifteen is too old to play."

"Oh, Son"—this was almost a groan—"Son, don't say that."

"Why, Father? Isn't fifteen a man?"

"Yes. Of course," said Father, bending over the sheet. How can I tell him, he thought, that there are no more boys such as he was three years ago? Boys, full of fun, playing games under an unclouded sky, living from day to day, carefree, like puppies. Boys who hadn't been forced into manhood to see this waste, this inhuman struggle; boys such as my little Jancsi was only three years ago. . . .

He couldn't tell him that. He only wrote: "Age preferred, twelve."

"And the girls?" He turned to Jancsi again. "I'm getting three of each kind," he smiled.

"Oh, I don't care. Make them small, smaller than Kate and Lily. Little ones who still respect a man. How soon can we get them?" he asked eagerly.

"How soon will they come?" Mother asked each day, impatiently.

"How soon?" Kate and Lily wanted to know as they sorted out clothes, shoes, small boots, and toys for the unknown children.

"Li'l' German come?" Nicolai and Sergei and Stana and Grigori and the two Peters came to look in the wagon every day. "One li'l' German for one big Russian?"

The coming of six hungry children was far more important than the news that a new menace had crushed all hope for an early peace. America, the country across the ocean, was sending men into the war too. It made little difference now which side of the warring forces America would help; a new, fresh power in the war between almost exhausted adversaries could only prolong the agony of all.

And so, at the end of June, almost on the day when the first American troops landed in France to be thrown into the maws of the war, six towheaded little Germans arrived on a Hungarian farm, to be nursed back into health and strength.

After the fresh troops went into action, an American general in Flanders wrote in his book: "Lost ten thousand men. Advanced three miles." Mother was writing too. She wrote:

Lottie, six years old, weighs 35 pounds
Marie, six years old, weighs 37
Pauline, six years old, weighs 40
Hans, twelve years old, weighs 65
Paul, twelve years old, weighs 70
Johann, eleven years old, weighs 62

When on July 6, 1917, the general sent a cable to Washington, he said: "Plans should contemplate sending over at least one million men by next May."

Mother wrote in her book on the same day: "All gained at least two pounds."

On July 17 the general wrote: "Plans for the future should be based on at least three million men."

On that day Mother said to Father: "I have stopped weighing them. They are gaining like little piglets."

Of these two, keeping records, Mother was far the happier.

CHAPTER X

SIX LITTLE GERMANS

Not that Mother didn't have her hands full. The day Father and Jancsi drove in with a wagonful of pale, frightened children, and for weeks afterward, the house was in an uproar most of the time. Lottie, Marie, Pauline, Hans, Paul, and Johann sat in the wagon like six bedraggled little birds, looking, with eyes far too large for their small, peaked faces, at this crowd of husky strangers. Strangers laughing as no one in Germany had laughed for a very long time. "What is there to laugh about?" their eyes seemed to ask while their pale lips began to twitch with the first sign of a wholesale crying bout.

211

It had not been so very bad in the town where the train had left them, because there was a man who spoke their language. In the village there was a very old little man in the funny little store who gave them candies and the few words of German he could remember. Driving along the lane with the large old trees on both sides had been nice because one never knew where it would end and one wanted to find out. But now . . . there were no German words to greet them, the candy was gone, there were only big, husky, laughing strangers at the end of the road, babbling in a strange, loud language.

Grigori, Nicolai, Sergei, Stana, and the two Peters, because they were the biggest of all, crowded everyone away from the wagon. "Li'l' German come to big Russian," roared Grigori in his friendliest roar, which meant the loudest, holding out hands that looked like giant's paws to the little Germans.

That was the last straw. Lottie started to howl and then the whole wagonful dissolved in tears, some silent, others very noisy.

"Mama . . . Mama," was the only word everyone understood.

"Come, darlings," cried Mother, on the verge of tears herself, "I am Mama now." She pointed to herself. "Mama."

"Well, so am I," Mari fought through the crowd, holding up three-year-old baby Panni, hoping that her smiling face would reassure the others. But baby Panni discovered her love, Gogi, and started to howl for him to hold her.

"I've nursed quite a bunch of my own"—little Grandma pushed her head between Sergei and Nicolai—"and I am not too old to take on one or two more."

"Here, you big bears, let me through!" Lily's mother, with the first show of real spirit since she came, poked thin elbows into Russian sides bulging with muscle. "You are enough to frighten any child out of his wits. Roaring at them like . . . like lions!"

Sergei was insulted. "Sergei no roar! Li'l' German no 'fraid. Li'l' German love big Russian, huh?" he asked with a grin that spread from ear to ear, tickling a shaking little German into fresh convulsions.

Something 'way in the back of Lily's mind was stirring. She had had German lessons in the finishing school and now she tried to drag words out of the oblivion into which they had fallen. She marched up to Grigori and gave him a downright order: "You pick me up. High! Higher! Now . . . hold still!"

"Here! *Hören!* . . . You . . . little . . . *zuhören!*" she shrieked over the din. One German word had acted like oil on troubled waters and six pairs of streaming eyes over six open mouths paid attention.

"*Nicht heulen! Dummkopf, nicht heulen. Gute Leute. Milch, Schinken, Brot . . . alles im Haus. Komm . . . fressen.* Don't howl, silly ones. Good people. Milk, ham, bread . . . everything in the house. Come and eat."

"Well, I never!" Grandma beamed in the sudden silence, her head still caught between Sergei and Nicolai. "They are beginning to smile . . . upon my soul they are."

"Sure!" Nicolai beamed back at the first pale smile in one little German face. "*Nich' heule'.*"

"*Milch?*" Marie and Pauline sniffed a wet and hopeful sniff because they had no handkerchiefs and even the name of milk called for an unhampered nose. In this lull of the storm Mother got another inning. "Mama," she repeated, pointing at the other women in turn. Another sniff, another smile.

"*Sechs Mama für sechs* . . ." Lily's idea was to tell them, while the telling was good, that there were six mothers for six children but "children" wouldn't come in German. So she called the six prospective mothers for inspection. "Mother, Grandma, Mari, Aunt Kormos, Kate"—she pointed each one out, then jabbed at herself—"and Lily."

Hans was really looking at her now. There was a real smile on his face. "*Danke, Lily. Wo . . . wo ist der Schinken?*"

"What's all this palaver? I want to *know*," Grandma demanded. Lily slipped off Grigori's arm. "He wants to know where the ham is. I said there was ham and bread and milk in the house. *Kommen!* Come." She waved to the now hopeful little crowd. They came into the house, following Lily between two lines of small and big strangers. Lily stopped in the middle of the kitchen.

"*Schinken, Brot, Milch!*" She swept her arm toward the loaded table as if she were a fairy with a magic wand.

"*Aaaach.*" And that was all the sound there was out of six little Germans until there was no ham, no bread, no milk left. They were oblivious of all the strangers who crowded into the kitchen and stood around beaming, whispering among themselves.

"If you don't stop them, Mother," Father chuckled after a long while, "they'll come apart at the seams." But she only smiled. "Let them. I'll sew them up again, with more."

"Li'l' German sure has big belly!" Nicolai beamed with admiration. "Li'l' German like li'l' Russian . . . eat like li'l' pig."

"All same." Kate winked at him. Grigori heard her. He gazed up at the strings of sausages hanging from the ceiling. He had heard of Kate's love for sausages. Jancsi had told him that Kate had eaten a couple of yards of them the first night she came to the farm. Now he said, bursting with suppressed laughter: "Sure. Li'l' German, li'l' Russian, all same, eat like li'l' pig. Li'l' devil no same. She eat like *two* li'l' pig. Grigori know." His own witticism seemed so funny to him that he let out one roar of laughter and forks clattered out of surprised little German hands.

"Shut up, Grigori." Kate pinched his arm. "Oh, the saints preserve us, they are at it again! See what you have done. . . ."

Grigori clapped his hand against his mouth and mumbled between his fingers: "Me fix." Lily rose to the occasion. "*Nicht heulen!* Don't howl." She pointed directly at Hans, who seemed the calmest. Hans nodded, half smiling, and spoke reassuringly to the others. After a suspicious glance or two and a few trembling sighs, they proceeded to finish what was left on the table. In the meantime Grigori herded Stana, Sergei, Nicolai, and the two Peters out of the room, whispering to them in Russian. It must have been a good whisper because amusement lay thick on their faces. In a short time guffaws

like muffled explosions proclaimed their return. Pushing everyone aside, they filed in. Six little German faces lifted appre-
hensively to break into smiles. Because in big Russian arms
were things far smaller and weaker than the little Germans
and even these small and weak things didn't seem afraid. The
two Peters had baby lambs, Nicolai had kittens peeking out
of both hands, so had Stana and Sergei. In the capacious nest
of Grigori's interlaced fingers downy yellow baby chicks were
swarming. Just Came, the mother cat, brought up the tail end
of the procession, her own tail waving a question-mark of
friendliness.

After the first surprised grumble of "Let's bring in the
cows and the horses too!" even Jancsi had to admit that Grigori
had found the shortest way into little German hearts. Because
in a miraculously short time six big Russians and six crooning,
smiling little Germans were in a huddle on the floor, protecting
downy baby chicks from the playful but far from downy
paws of tiny kittens and both chicks and kittens from awkward, prancing feet of baby lambs.

"Who would have thought of that!" sighed Jancsi when a
chorus of giggles and booming laughs filled the kitchen and
wet sniffs sounded peaceful, like raindrops falling off trees
after the rain has stopped. Grigori, quite busy with two kittens sharpening claws in his beard, and Marie making it worse
by pulling their tails, took time to answer Jancsi.

"Grigori think," he mumbled. "Grigori know that li'l' thing
love li'l' thing. All same, Jancsi . . . li'l' Russian, li'l' German,
li'l' Hungarian . . . all same to Grigori."

"Sure." Sergei nodded wisely and tickled the same little German into laughter who, an hour ago, had howled at the sight of him. "Comrade . . . huh?"

This was another word they all knew, young and old, Hungarian, German, and Russian, and as they repeated the word the old kitchen seemed to glow with the spirit of it. Comrade. Friend.

But in spite of the good food, the "li'l' things," the sunshine and care surrounding them, the little Germans had a hard time with homesickness. There were many evenings when bedtime was a bedlam of sobs, tantrums, a flood of tears. All the tenderness of six volunteer mamas, six clowning Russians, all Father's and Grandpa's smiles (and sometimes shouts), Jancsi's wholehearted friendliness, couldn't make up for the mamas and papas so far away in Germany. Letters came and went, marking the passing weeks of summer and fall. Letters to Germany were written by Hans, Paul, and Johann; they wrote for the little girls too. Slowly these letters grew more cheerful, more voluble, as the infinite small details of life on this friendly place became the life of six little Germans.

"These people," wrote Hans in the late fall of 1917, "do not hate anyone. In our school in Berlin we were told that Russians and English and French are monsters. That is not true, Mother. The six Russians, especially my best friend Stana, are like German men, like Papa. They like to laugh and play with us and they like to work. Maybe the French and English men are the same. Our teacher told us a lie about the

Jews too. Herr Mandelbaum, the storekeeper in the village, is not selfish and rich and bad. He is very old and small and he has lost two sons in the war. Herr Nagy, Jancsi's father, is giving him money now to pay for goods in the store because Herr Mandelbaum has no more left. He bought war bonds to help the country. If he is helping Hungary, isn't he helping Germany too? We are allies. And nobody in the village pays him for anything and he does not keep books. He just remembers what people owe him, Jancsi says, but now he often forgets because people have no money. I cannot understand Hungarian very well yet, but Jancsi can make me understand many things.

"I do not hate Russians now, Mother, and I think that Jews are very kind and good. When I grow up I want to be a teacher and teach what Grigori is always saying. He says that people are all the same in Russia and Germany and Hungary and that we are all brothers. It's true, Mother. Why did our teacher in Berlin lie to us? I have asked Herr Nagy, but he said our teacher must have been a stupid man. If he is stupid, Mother, why is he a teacher?

"But sometimes I think that maybe Herr Nagy and Grigori are wrong. Because if we *are* all brothers, why is there a war?

"Please, Mother, tell me who is right?"

When the letter came with the answer, the three blond heads of Hans, Paul, and Johann bent over it eagerly. Maybe this would tell them who is right.

"My dear little Hans," the letter said, "I am glad that you are well and happy. Please tell Herr Nagy and your Russian friends that a German mother is praying for them every night. Tell them that I want to thank them for teaching my boy to love instead of to hate.

"Forget all your teacher in Berlin has told you. Be very good, little Hans, to deserve the kindness and love of those good people.

"Papa is still in the war in France. Here is a snapshot he sent last month. This is all I can send you for Christmas this year . . . and all my love. . . ."

"*Weihnachten* . . . Christmas," Johann sighed and there might have been another cry but Jancsi called in from the yard:

"Hey! The horses are waiting! Let's have some fun!"

"Pretty good," he conceded as he surveyed the almost perfect posture of Hans, Johann, and Paul on horseback. Father had let him bring three broken-in horses from the corrals and teach the boys to ride.

"I'll make horsemen out of you yet. Come on, we'll ride to the village and back. Sit up straight, you . . . you questionmark!" He glowered at Paul. "Toes in, elbows hugging your sides, head up. There!"

"*Jawohl*." Johann grinned at him. "*Jawohl*, Herr Brigadier General Jancsi!"

"None of that. I am not a soldier. I am a horseman. And speak Hungarian to me, or you'll stay home."

"You tell him, Jancsi . . . you tell him!" came the voice of Nicolai from the barn. "He sit on horse like cow . . . all hump. He speak like wagonwheel on stone . . . all noise."

There he was, gesticulating wildly, but the mile-wide grin on his face belied his scolding words. They all loved the little Germans, Jancsi most of all. Especially these boys, to whom a horse was a prancing miracle on four legs, and Jancsi master of the wildest of horses, a hero. He could show off to this uncritical audience who didn't know enough to notice that when the horse stood on its hind legs as if it were trying to throw him off, it was Jancsi who pulled the reins. He couldn't get away with this when Kate was around because she called his bluff. But the German boys shared his attitude of mild scorn toward mere girls, and if Kate tried to criticize their hero, three blank faces looked through her as if she were thin air. And that made Kate simply furious.

"You wait . . . you just wait, you conceited little monkeys. I'll show you and you too, big smarty! Just you wait!"

One day, a bright, sunny day in early December, she held a long, secret conversation with Mother. "There'll be no living with them if we women don't do something. Just this once more, Auntie, please!" she pleaded when Mother didn't show the proper co-operation. "Let me ride once more the way I used to, like a boy, and then I won't mind being an almost grown-up girl. Just to show them!"

"All right, lamb." Mother kissed her. "Go ahead and I'll keep my fingers crossed, hoping that you will win." ("And that there won't be any broken bones to mend," she sighed to herself.)

"Humph. I know I will. On Milky? There isn't a horse in Jancsi's herd who can beat Milky."

"I'll make it more interesting," Mother proposed. "The one who wins can have all the fresh sausages he can hold, for once."

"It'll be a 'she,' not a 'he,' Auntie. You wait and see."

There was more secret conversation with Grigori and so, when it was time for Jancsi and the boys to leave—they had a long ride planned for that day—five horses came prancing out of the stable. Bársony, three chestnuts for the German boys, and Milky. Snow-white, beautiful with the red saddle and reins studded with brass, Milky pawed like a colt.

"Now then." Kate marched up to the surprised gang of so superior small men. She looked like a tall, lovely boy herself, wearing Jancsi's pleated pants and short, braided jacket. "I'll race you to the end of the lane and back. The one who gets home first can have sausages"—she held out her arms in a wide gesture—"yards and yards and yards."

This was *one* weakness the boys shared with her. "*Würste?* Sausages?" beamed Hans, Paul, and Johann.

"Yes. You can watch me eat them. I'll show you what a girl can do." Kate was in the saddle with one smooth leap.

"Humph," Jancsi said. "We'll show you, smarty." But he wasn't so sure as he sounded. Kate could ride almost as well as he, there was no denying that. Hadn't he taught her himself? Now he was pinning his hope on the "almost" and the fact that Kate hadn't been riding very much—just enough to keep Milky exercised.

Word had gone around that something exciting was going on and everyone came to see them start off. Grigori bellowed according to Kate's directions: "One . . . twooooo . . . go!"

The "go" sounded like an explosion and spurs were not needed to make the horses go. They tore out of the yard and into the lane and out of sight between the trees. How they rode! Kate was taking long, gasping breaths of joy, the boys were shouting, Jancsi laughed aloud as he had not laughed since he was a boy of thirteen. And he was ahead, 'way ahead by the time they neared the end of the lane. Those boys could ride too, the conceited little rascals, Kate groaned to herself.

"Milky," she gasped as she made a wide circle around the last trees in the lane, "Milky, help me. Run, Milky, run! *Run!* This is the last time, Milky. I'll be a big girl tomorrow . . . I promised Auntie." She was talking in gasps and maybe Milky understood, because the distance between Jancsi and Kate seemed to shorten and . . . now she was passing one . . . two . . . three horses.

"Come, Milky, dear Milky!" Kate cried as the white house gleamed up between the trees. Milky's hoofs were pounding the frozen road furiously, but still Jancsi was 'way ahead.

"Wheeeeeeeee!" came the ear-splitting tin-whistle scream of a little girl who was to be big, almost grown-up Kate to-morrow. "Wheeeeee!"

This time Jancsi wasn't pulling the reins when Bársony reared to paw the air with thrashing front hoofs. "Down, Bársony!" he shouted and tightened the hold of his knees. In a moment he was leaping ahead again but that one moment had been enough for Kate and Milky. They flew by him, through the gate, and into the yard. Jancsi was on their heels but Kate had won.

Four panting, defeated boys and a disheveled, boyish-looking girl stood glaring at one another.

"That wasn't fair!" gasped Jancsi. "You screamed."

"Pfff. I got ahead of *them* without screaming," Kate retorted hotly. "And you had spurs on, I didn't. So there! Was it a fair race?" She turned to the three boys.

"*Ja, ja.* Fair race," Hans admitted, very reluctantly. He shrugged and turned to Paul and Johann. "Kate has sausage. *Kein Wurst für uns.*"

"Who said so? I don't want any," Kate said unexpectedly. "You eat the sausages, boys; and . . . and you can ride . . . awfully well for . . . *little* boys."

She ran into the house to change, perfectly satisfied now to grow up, beginning tomorrow, because Hans had shouted after her: "You ride better than many boys."

After this, Christmas seemed only a few "sleeps" away. Grigori had started counting days by "sleeps" and now they were all doing it.

"Johann sleep five, then Christmas!"

"Pauline sleep two, Christmas."

Then there were no more "sleeps" left and it was Christmas Eve again, the fourth Christmas of the war. The old kitchen glowed once more with candles on the tree, their mellow light shining onto many more faces than ever before. There were toys for the little ones under the tree, made by Grandpa, Father, and the Russians. There were letters and photographs from Germany, France, Russia. It was a haven, a charmed spot, this old kitchen. Old walls embracing people who had been blown there by a terrible storm, giving them refuge, peace, and happiness for a little while. Perhaps another storm would blow them far apart, but now they were together.

After the candles had burned down and it was time to go to bed, Hans reached up to the shelf and took down his father's picture. "*Gute Nacht, lieber Papa, schlaf wohl.* Good night, dear Father, sleep well," he whispered.

He didn't know then, and wouldn't know for many weeks, that his father was then sleeping under a white blanket of snow somewhere in France.

CHAPTER XI

THE SINGING TREE

"Time goes so fast," Mother sighed one evening in April . . . April 1918. "The apple tree is showing white; time to thin out my tomato seedlings in the boxes."

"Time . . . there are so many ways to count the time now," Kate said in a puzzled voice. "Remember, Auntie, when I came to you six years ago, we used to say the same thing: 'Time for the tomato seedlings, the apple tree is showing white.' Later it was time to plant the flower garden because

231

old mother stork was sitting on her eggs. Time for the gypsies was time to dig potatoes in the fall, and when the first snow came it was time to bring out the spinning-wheel and the loom for winter evenings.

"Now, I count the time by Daddy's letters. Grigori counts them by sleeps; so do the little children. Hans counts them from the day he . . . he heard about his father. Uncle Márton, you count them by what the newspapers say about the war, Mari by little Panni's age and teeth, Jancsi by the foals. Grandpa waits for the time when they can go back. Lily . . . oh, all of us in all different ways. All except you, Auntie. You . . . oh, I'm all mixed up now . . ."

She looked around, a little ashamed of this long and slightly incoherent speech. There had been something in her mind she wanted to put into words but with the words coming so slowly the idea had flown.

Uncle Márton was looking at her intently with a very small but very warm smile. They were sitting around the kitchen table, Father, Mother, Grandpa, Grandma, Jancsi, Lily and her Mother, Mari and Kate. The Russians were out in the yard, singing softly to the achy little tune Grigori was playing on his balalaika. The six German children had gone to bed; some with toys, some with forbidden but overlooked kittens (new kittens, all spoken for), and Hans with an ache in his heart that even a kitten could not purr away.

"I don't think you are mixed up, Kate," said Father, still with the warm smile on his face. "I think I know what you were thinking and it's about time somebody put it into words.

Let me tell you a story. It will be a war story again. It begins with guns booming and shells screaming, but it will end with the words you were thinking.

"This story began one day in August 1915. We had been advancing all night . . . all through the long, silent night that followed a day of the heaviest shellfire from both lines, the Russians' and ours. Each had been trying to advance. Finally the Russians left their trenches and retreated. After sundown we were ordered to follow their retreat. We marched or rather crept and crawled and stumbled across this no-man's land of shell holes, barbed wire, burned-down forests, ruined houses, and deserted Russian gun-nests. Except for us, there was nothing alive anywhere. No rabbits scurrying underfoot, no squirrels jumping from tree to tree, no birds, not even an owl hooting, for miles around. Just odds and ends of broken things the war leaves behind.

"All night we crept and crawled and stumbled and still there was only dark night and silence to greet us. Even gunfire would have been welcome in that night, anything to break the spell of having come into a land where only we, creeping men, were alive.

"And then, when men's teeth began to chatter with fear far more benumbing than fear of injury or death, a finger of light, a tiny, weak herald of the approaching dawn, shivered on the edge of darkness, grew less weak, then stronger, changed from gray-green into the palest of yellow streaks across the horizon, turned into gold, then orange, and at last we could see again.

" 'Dawn,' a creeping man said as if he had never hoped to see a dawn again.

"Ahead of us and behind us lay a devastated forest with only skeletons of trees still standing here and there. Underfoot there was the same litter of broken things we had come to know by touch, if not by sight . . . barbed wire, broken guns, empty cartridges, empty tins. All around us was the same silence that had roared in our ears all night.

"And then, as the sun broke through the clouds at last, we saw one tree. One single apple tree that must have been near a house; only the house was no longer there.

" 'It is alive,' a creeping man said, but with the words he rose. 'Alive,' another man said as if he never hoped to see a green tree again.

" 'It sings,' someone whispered. 'It is alive. I can hear it.'

"Now men rose to their feet and walked and ran like *men,* toward the singing tree, which was alive with birds . . . living birds singing to the dawn in a live apple tree. Birds. Little wrens and sparrows, late robins, warblers, thrushes, orioles . . . the green tree was alive with birds all singing . . . singing to the dawn.

"Against the trunk, owls huddled sleepily; there were jackdaws, and even a crow or two had taken shelter there. Friends and foes of the bird world, side by side, all from different nests, nests that perhaps would never shelter them again, for nests must have fallen with the trees that held them. And here they were, small, feathered orphans of a man-made storm, huddled together on a green apple tree, singing to the dawn.

"Perhaps they too were merely passing time until it would be safe to travel forth and build anew, or seek the old nests. Just passing time, but while they waited, each was singing a song to dawn and each in a different way.

"The one live thing that would never go away unless a man-made gun should uproot it from the earth it grew in was the apple tree. It did not *wait* for time to pass. It did not try to sing. It just *was* what God had made it, a simple, homy tree. Small orphans . . . large ones . . . for a while found shelter on its sturdy limbs. . . . They would pass on. . . ."

Father was looking at Mother now and laid his hand on hers folded on the table. "They would pass on. New ones might come. There might be storms again. But she . . . *she*, mother of all, she would remain the same." He said the last words in a husky voice, looking into Mother's eyes.

The cuckoo-clock on the shelf sounded very loud. It had the whole kitchen to itself and made the best of it while human beings kept their silence. Then there was a long, tremulous sigh from Kate that sounded as if she had been holding her breath for too long. Grandpa immediately cleared his throat as only old men can who are very young and soft inside and want to cover it up with a big noise. "Grrrumph! You might as well tell me, Márton . . . am I the blinking owl or the crow?"

To the little awakening smiles that followed his question, Grandma added a chuckle: "Turning my daughter's head, that's what the man is doing. Never saw the like of him for flowery language. Humph! What's a woman for, if not to take care of those who need her? Isn't she big enough? Next thing you know, I'll have to put a gusset into that bodice of hers, it's fair bursting now!"

They were all laughing now. Lily's mother leaned forward a moment later and touched Father's sleeve. "Márton . . . that finger of light heralding the dawn, might the Russian Revolution be that first pale light of hope?"

"I think so," Father said seriously. "At any rate, this much is certain: there is no more organized Russian army fighting against us or the Germans. It might . . . might mean that . . ."

"War will be over?" asked Jancsi. "Soon?"

"Daddy . . . Daddy would come home, then. . . . Oh, Uncle Márton!"

"And our daddy." Lily's mother smiled at her daughter. "And Peter." She patted Mari's hand. All their eyes were turned now toward the shivering, pale, small finger of light, the light of new hope . . . it might bring on the dawn.

Everywhere eyes of men, women, and children were turning toward the same light of hope. The prayer for peace in people's hearts lent it a radiance it never really had. For the collapse of Russia, while it was the beginning of the end of war, also unleashed another menace on mankind—class hatred.

But war was still spinning its mad whirlwind in the west. France, England, Germany, Italy were writhing in the terrific final struggles of 1918, and millions of Americans were thrown into it. Austrian and Hungarian troops were pouring from north to south, to the Italian front. Tired troops, bedraggled troops, rebellious troops. Veterans of four years who had reached the ragged edge of human endurance. Young boys who, when the war began, had been children of fifteen, six-teen. Tired old men and bewildered youngsters, all of them desperately wanting one thing only, to go home. Go home. Go home.

Who cared now about victory? What was victory? Which of the exhausted nations could ever feel victorious? Who would dare to parade with brass bands and flags flying over millions of graves?

Medals were showered on these men all over Europe. Medals from staggering governments, in one last effort to keep their armies together. Haha, laughed the men all over Europe. So they are giving us little shiny toys to play with. Maybe they think that little shiny toys will make us forget that we are hungry and ragged. And afraid. Afraid of ghostly eyes star-ing at us in our dreams and ghostly lips asking: Why did you kill me, Brother?

And so the end came. The end of war. The end of the Habsburg Empire. The end of the German Empire. Nobody cared. It was the *end of war*.

And with the end of war came a voice from across the ocean, the voice of an American President. In the dreadful hush that lay over Europe after the guns had ceased to roar, this voice sounded like a clarion call, proclaiming a new, happier day.

"Impartial justice to all . . . in the common interest of all the nations. . . ."

These words had reached the small Hungarian village late in the fall of 1918, together with the first ragged, tired men returning home. Together with the news that the exchange of prisoners between the nations had begun.

Father and Jancsi drove into the village that day for the news. When they entered the store, Uncle Moses came to meet them with outstretched hands. "Oh, Márton . . . Márton," he almost sobbed the words, "read this paper. Read what the American President has said. Read, Márton, and rejoice!"

They read. When they finished the long article, so full of the high ideals of a man who wanted only justice, equality, peace, everlasting peace for all men because all men were created equal, the big farmer and the small storekeeper looked at each other with shining eyes. Uncle Moses pointed with trembling fingers to the paper. "This, Márton, this makes me sure now . . . for the first time *sure,* that Joseph and Sam have not died in vain. A new day is coming, Márton, for us, for all nations. No more wars, Márton. No more persecution, no more intolerance ever. . . ."

He was trembling and very pale. Father rose and put his arms around him, gently, as if he were holding a child.

"No more, Uncle Moses. I am just as happy as you are. But you look very tired. You haven't had a rest in years and years, neither has Aunt Sarah. Come out with us to the farm for a few days. The store will get along without you."

Uncle Moses shook his head. "No, thank you, dear friend. Aaron might be home any day. We want to be home to welcome our lawyer son. Only," he smiled, "Aaron won't be a big lawyer now, as we have planned. No. You know what he wants to be?"

"What, Uncle Moses?"

"The fourth Mandelbaum keeping store in the village. A smart man like Aaron, a storekeeper." Uncle Moses shook his head ruefully, but his eyes were dancing. "I'll have a hard time teaching him. . . ."

"How to swap silver buttons for a cow, or a cow for wool, or wool for harness, with some glasses and a whip thrown in?" Jancsi laughed.

"No," chuckled Uncle Moses. "That'll come easy. But it will take time to teach him . . . *when* to forget what people owe him. Nobody can learn that out of books."

Father held out his hand. "I am glad, Uncle Moses. Very glad. Jancsi will learn to be a real farmer now"—he laughed at Jancsi's indignant frown—"a *real* farmer who milks his own cows instead of letting a mere girl do it for him. Aaron will learn to be the kind of storekeeper we always had here, and between the big farm and the small store, people will live again and work again and sing again."

On the way home, when they reached the lane, Jancsi touched Father's arm. "Could we stop for a moment, Father? I would like to see if it's still there." He pointed toward the tree where four years ago he had seen the ancient post of 1848. "The . . . the monument."

Father stopped the horses without a word. Then, as they were walking to the tree, he smiled at Jancsi. "If it isn't, Son, you and I will carve a new one. For the next generations to see."

But it was there. Four years of storms could not mar the

deeply carved words that had withstood the storms of half
a century.

"Liberty, equality, fraternity," and underneath, the list of
names beginning with Márton Nagy, the large landowner, and
ending with Moses Mandelbaum, the small Jewish merchant.

"Liberty, equality, fraternity," Father read the words slowly. "Soon they will ring again all over the world, these beautiful
words. Only a fourth one, just born, will ring clearer. *Peace*."

He looked up into the November sky. "Please God. Just
peace."

In silence they walked to the wagon again. Driving between
the old trees that had led him home so often, Jancsi sighed.
"Lily's mother said once that these trees seemed to whisper:
'Come, we'll lead you home.' Kate came home this way. . . .
Lily, Mari, baby Panni, the Russians, the six little sniffing Germans. . . . Now it will be strange to see most of them go the
other way. The house will be too large for us."

"The trees will lead Uncle Sándor home soon," said Father
and smiled down on Jancsi, "and unless I miss my guess, he
won't come home alone."

Jancsi was taken aback for a moment. Then he grinned.
"Sonia?"

"Uhum. What do you think, Son?"

"Another woman. That's what I think."

"Well, Son, you and I will stick together. That's enough,
isn't it?"

Jancsi sighed a deep, big sigh, from deep down in his heart.
"Yes. That's enough."

They drove on, lost in thought for a while. Then when the white house gleamed up between the trees, Jancsi spoke. "You know what, Father?"

"What, Son?"

"That story about the singing tree . . . remember?"

"Uhum."

"Well, I knew what you meant about Mother and how she is always the same . . . and I liked the way you said the story for her. But . . . but to me . . . the singing tree was more than . . . more than even Mother. To me . . ."

"Yes?"

"To me the stillness and the ruins in the story were the . . . was the time when . . . you weren't here. And the tree . . . it's the house and you and Mother . . . it's everything we are, so of together. Aw . . . you know what I mean. . . ."

Father had his arm around Jancsi's shoulder and spoke low, happy voice:

"Small orphans, big ones, for a while found shelter. .

"They would pass on . . ." Jancsi said slowly.

"New ones might come. There might be storm but . . ." Father waited for Jancsi to finish:

"But we, the house and us, we would remain th